FLACCI

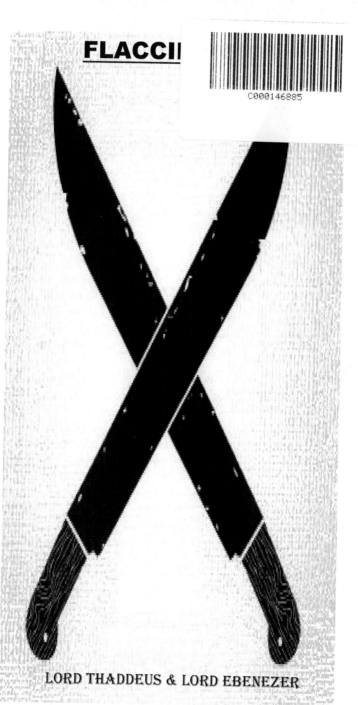

LORD THADDEUS & LORD EBENEZER

"For my ex-wife, may she forever burn in hell".

TABLE OF CONTENTS

CHAPTER 1: KUDOS TO THE COLONEL.

Location: London

Date: June 10th, 2035

Time: 21:30hrs

Night had fallen on the city of London like a fat slimy turd, on an empty street the dim lights of a 1958 Ford Zephyr could slowly be seen patrolling a destitute neighbourhood of the city, this particular area had a bad reputation for crime, especially at nightfall and already loud echoing screams could be heard coming from a nearby dark alleyway, it seems like some fat shitheel was attempting to have his way with some sobbing dame as usual. You see since the wheel of society stopped turning it was just another night for most women in these streets, a night filled with terror where nowhere was safe and dangerous things lurked in the shadows, however this time it was going to be different, the screams wouldn't last long as unbeknownst to the reeking scoundrel that had the sobbing woman by her throat, the Espartano brothers had already arrived on the scene, the hulking muscle bound figures exited the Zephyr and quietly shut the doors, Ebenezer was the slightly larger of the two standing at roughly seven foot tall, A true skyscraper of a man, an enormous Mohawk protruded from his cranium, his cybernetic hand was malfunctioning as usual, spinning around at the wrist at an incredible speed, he promptly smashed against a nearby wall levelling a house and correcting the error, a poverty stricken family emerged from the ruins in tatters and Ebenezer shrugged, "whatever" he muttered whilst producing a fresh pack of Drexel's from his canary yellow waistcoat "ready to rock?" he said whilst handing his brother Thaddeus a cigarette, Thaddeus graciously accepted the cigarette and used his cybernetic eye laser to light it "did you scan the alley?" Ebenezer asked "scan complete" Thaddeus replied as he took a large drag "John McDermott, 52 years old, sewage factory employee, bro hes got previous" he said as his shoulder mounted environment scanner retracted back into its armoured housing. Ebenezer took the cigarette from his mouth and flicked it into the ruins of the house, "let's roll!" he said as the house went up in flames.

Slowly the two enormous men slipped into the entrance of the alleyway, their chrome body Armor shone majestically in the oily light of a nearby condom machine and with the stealth of a cat they began creeping up on the assailant like a post vindaloo bowel movement...

"Bitch quit your wining and give me some honey before I crack your fucking skull!" John McDermott yelled sadistically at the helpless woman".

She whimpered as the thug pulled a leather strapped Cosh from his pocket and raised his hand to the night sky "fuck it, maybe this will shut you up" but before he could bring down his tool...

Swoooosshhhhhhh!!!

From the shadows Ebenezer's mighty golden machete cut through the air, whizzing unstoppably down the alleyway faster than the late great Andre the Giant could chug a beer, it instantly severed the filthy rapist's paw like a hot knife through butter, the woman dropped to the ground, the severed hand still holding onto her throat, blood jetted from the stump as she threw it aside with a horrified scream. The fat monstrosity bellowed in pain and fell to his knees, he clutched his stump which was now pissing blood all over his stained string vest, he looked up just in time to see Thaddeus standing above him, his half cyborg face twisted into a vicious smile, he suddenly thrust a solid platinum blunderbuss directly into the rapists groin, he let out another blood curdling scream as with an enormous bang his filthy uncircumcised member was blown clean from his body, Thaddeus threw his head back in laughter as he pulled his own machete from its holster and held it to the thugs dirty face, its gorgeous engraved blade which read "death to dildo man" glinted wonderfully in the moonlight.

"Well?" Thaddeus asked the women who was clearly in a state of shock "wh... what!?" She stammered as she wiped blood from her face with the bottom of her skirt "what do you want us to do to this piece of shit?"

Ebenezer handed her a Drexel which she gladly accepted, he lit it for her with a lighter made of solid palladium and after a drag and a moments pause she exclaimed: "kill the son of a bitch! kill him like the animal he is!"

"Please!" the fat mess on the floor weakly begged as he writhed in his own blood which was now gushing at an incredible rate from his newfound vagina "disgusting" spat Ebenezer, "pig blood on my shoes!, I just had them polished" "dont worry bro" Thaddeus said cheerfully "I know what'll cheer you up" with that he took the woman by the arm and went to walk her out of the alleyway "hey bro?" Ebenezer called after him "where are you going?" Thaddeus turned and winked, "Oh I almost forgot!" the Woman called back to Ebenezer "thanks!" Ebenezer nodded and turned back to Mr rapist who was now sobbing and turning a brilliant shade of green "alone at last" Ebenezer grinned, "but dont worry, my brother will be back soon, no doubt hes just nipped to the Zephyr to grab something to really turn this place into pee pee pants city".

"Please, Please!!" Moaned lard ass "shush" Ebenezer said loudly back handing him across the face with a titanium fist and McDermott tasted blood once again "we both know it's too late for that you dirty mother fucker". Ebenezer turned with a smile as outside the alley a car boot slammed, Thaddeus's hulking silhouette appeared once again, his red laser eye visible in the darkness and as he walked the sound of a sloshing jerry can of petrol could be heard echoing through the blood-stained alleyway.

"Wha what's that for!?" the dickless creature gasped as Thaddeus gently swung the jerry can back and forth in front of his face, "what do you fucking think it's for!? Thaddeus suddenly yelled as he shoved the jerry can nozzle into the rapist's mouth "Ebenezer held him down as Thaddeus emptied the entire contents of the can down his throat into his fat stomach "gluurrk!! Haaaalp!!" Blurped the piece of shit, petrol spurting from his nose, "ugh! Bad manners!! Yelled Ebenezer, "I fucking hate bad manners!" And with that he pulled a meat cleaver from his shoulder holster, frantically hacking he sliced huge chunks of flesh from the rapists torso, all the while he laughed before standing up and re adjusting his gorgeous mohawk, "here catch" he said to Thaddeus chucking him his lighter, Thaddeus flicked the zippo and threw in onto the pile of blurping lard, the horrific screams of the burning sex pest quickly filled the air as he writhed pitifully on the ground "man I love this fucking job" exclaimed Ebenezer gleefully, "by the way what did you do with the chick?" he asked Thaddeus, Thaddeus grinned and patted the wallet sized bulge in his waist coat pocket "bro your too generous" Ebenezer said shaking his head "you know shell just spend it on more Zial" Thaddeus exhaled loudly vocalising his grim agreement. The burning man's flesh was now starting to melt from his face and the screams had now turned into harrowing shrieks "shut the fuck up!" Thaddeus suddenly yelled as he stomped his size 12 romper stompers into the rapist's head, Ebenezer sniggered as McDermott's eyeballs popped from his skull and finally all was silent. "thats better" he said blissfully, "listen Ebenezer, well get that fucking drug of the streets but I'll be honest with you, if we get to keep spending our evenings shelling out punishment like this, I'm in no rush" Ebenezer slapped his thigh and laughed in agreement.

The two brothers sat in the alleyway sipping whiskey from Ebenezer's hip flask having a jolly good laugh until the flames finally stopped "fuck me look even his skeleton was fat" Ebenezer chuckled "looks kinda like KFC" Thaddeus exclaimed suddenly grabbing his machete and hacking off a bit of crispy flesh. "what?" He asked Ebenezer whose mouth was open in disbelief "I missed supper" "ha ha you do make me laugh bro" Ebenezer chuckled as Thaddeus gobbled down a piece of Kentucky fried sex offender.

Thaddeus clicked his seatbelt on and Ebenezer set the Zephyr's aircon to rich, "right, back to the airship, I think, we could do with some refreshment" Ebenezer said cheerfully as the engine roared into life, with that he flipped an intercom switch on the dashboard and a robotic voice crackled over the speakers "uhh yes boss how can I help?", "goffbot, be prepared to lower the ramp well be there in fifteen" Thaddeus said loudly "uhh yes boss will lower the ramp now" the voice replied "no not now you fucking useless machine, when were closer!" Ebenezer said angrily "uhh roger boss" the voice replied. Ebenezer shook his head in disbelief "that fucking robot" he looked at Thaddeus who was now clutching his stomach and wincing, "what's up bro?" he asked, "ah nothing" Thaddeus replied, "I just need some rest my gutty wutts are killing me".

"You know what you can do to stop that dont you?" Ebenezer said holding back a smirk, "what?" Thaddeus replied.

"Stay off the junk food".

The wheels screeched as Ebenezer punched the accelerator to the floor and the Zephyr launched down the street at an incredible speed. Thaddeus observed through the window and watched as on every street corner the various Zial dealers fled at the sight of the brother's car. "Jesus" Thaddeus exclaimed "this fucking place gets worse every night "Id like to find out who makes this fucking drug throw them into a jet engine", Ebenezer laughed and nodded in agreement, "we will bro" he replied.

"we will."

CHAPTER 2: THE CURIOUS DEMISE OF DILDO MAN MCKELLAR.

Location: the "Hungry Bird" airship.

Date: June 10th, 2035

Time: 21:45hrs

The huge iron ramp of the airship slammed shut as Ebenezer engaged the polished chrome handbrake of the Zephyr, "were moving out, engage the turbines" Thaddeus said loudly into the intercom "uhh ok boss firing up the impellers now" the synthetic voice of the airships useless robot replied.

"Couple of whiskeys I reckon?" Ebenezer said thoughtfully. "When in Rome" Thaddeus replied.

The two men exited the vehicle and were immediately greeted by the ship's mechanic, a huge musclebound tattooed Fijian man by the name of Waqa waqa. "hey, hey mother fuckers" the giant said as he slapped the two brothers a high five each "how's the car holding up?", "fucking amazing as always thanks to you" Thaddeus replied over the sounds of the airship's turbines starting up "joining us for a drink tonight mate?" Ebenezer asked as they walked toward the deck lift "fuck yeah, you know me man, I never miss a party" Waqa replied eagerly "as soon as I refuel the zephyr I'll be on my way. "we'll pour you a cold one" Ebenezer called as the two men entered the lift "shit you do remember the last time he drank with us dont you?" Thaddeus enquired "we were out for a fucking week, and the airship was trashed, the guys an animal" "yeah" Ebenezer replied as he attempted to adjust his mechanical hand which was spinning wildly out of control again "but he cooks a fucking hell of a hangover breakfast" Thaddeus looked with concern at his brother as his hand had begun smashing itself into the walls of the elevator "bro you should go and check in with Mya in the med bay, shell sort that out" Ebenezer nodded in agreement, "I will" he replied "but whiskey first obviously", "obviously" Thaddeus replied in utter agreement.

The doors to the airships lounge whooshed open and as usual the two brothers were met with the delightful sight of the rooms main attraction, adjacent to the rooms grand fireplace was the captured disgusting body of Fatty "dildo man" McKellar, and just in time too! he had started his nightly routine of pathetic blood

11

curdling shrieks and screams but luckily he could not be heard from outside of the Perspex box for two reasons: firstly because it was soundproof and secondly because his tongue had been ripped out of his mouth long ago, now with his own personal fish tank and just five centimetres of hydrofluoric acid to keep him company his body had decomposed stupendously, his deeply bloodshot eyes could just make out the two figures as they dumped their body armour and took their seats at the gorgeous mahogany table in the centre of the room, as usual he tried in vain to get the attention of the two men by frantically pounding his melted stumps against the glass but to no avail, Thaddeus and Ebenezer were already having too much of a jolly good time to give a shit about the hideous creature, but finally after the brothers had imbibed a few large glasses of delicious scotch he saw through lidless eyes that Thaddeus was pointing and laughing at him, he hung his head in despair as he longed for instant death but the two brothers would never make it that easy.. and boy didn't he know it.

"That fucking things looking at me again" Thaddeus exclaimed in disgust, Ebenezer turned around in his Kashmir lined oak armchair "we dont want to see your fucking ugly face!" He yelled, he turned back laughing and picked up his cigar "so?" He Asked Thaddeus, "blackjack or poker?" he reached for a pack of solid gold playing cards given to him personally by Elron Hubbard himself and started to open the pack, "neither" Thaddeus replied with a grin slowly spreading across his grid as his eyes focused on the dildo man.

"I want to play snap".

"Yes!" yelled Ebenezer pounding his enormous fist onto the table "my favourite game!" Fatty quivered in the corner of his box for he knew exactly what was about to happen, Ebenezer leapt up and strode across the room, grabbing a remote control from one of the many bookcases, he punched a button, the fireplace next to Fatty's Perspex prison revolved 180 degrees and was now replaced by a gunmetal wall covered in a million different buttons and levers. "you know" Thaddeus exclaimed cheerfully as he walked over to the wall "getting this installed has to be the best feature of the airship bro", "apart from the armoury of course" Ebenezer replied "well of course" Thaddeus agreed before raising his finger to the wall of buttons. "eeny meeny miny mo" he said loudly before stopping on a random red button "bro what does this one do?" he asked "ah ha I know what that one does" Ebenezer chuckled with glee "give it a whirl" Thaddeus looked down and smiled at Fatty who was shaking his head frantically, his pleading eyes wide with terror. Thaddeus pressed the button and observed with delight as multiple circular saw disks slowly emerged from slits inside of the box, the surgical steel blades whizzing at a ferocious speed, slowly but surely the blades cut into Fatty's flesh and his mouth stretched open to the point of dislocation. "Bro hit the button to your left with the speaker icon above it" Ebenezer said, "what this one?" Thaddeus replied pressing the button, a horrendous din suddenly filled the room as from the lounges surround sound speakers erupted a hell of a racket, the noise was indecipherable but one could suggest a combination of a pig squealing and the grinding of metal, Thaddeus gazed into the box and to his delight the splattering of blood tainted the Perspex viewing window, the dildo man's toothless gob hole had opened so wide the bottom jaw had indeed dislocated and now it swung loosely as he bellowed like a tortured warthog, the steel blades slicing deeper and deeper into his rotting flesh "fantastic!" exclaimed Thaddeus "I can't believe Ive never given this one a go" "it gets better" Ebenezer replied turning another dial

14

"you can adjust the tempo of the cutting depth so you could leave him like this for days if you wanted", "fucking awesome!" Thaddeus replied in a delighted tone, Thaddeus pressed the red button again and the blades slowly retracted dripping blood and chunks of flesh as they smoothly slid back into their housings. "I can't here myself fucking think!" yelled Ebenezer over the pigs wailing, he strode over and hit a button labelled mute and all was silent once more "thats better, right my turn" he said taking a generous swill from his glass.

Ebenezer had a particular love for this machine, he had employed a team of 10 or so ex NASA engineers to draw up the designs, after following a tip off he was able to personally capture the notorious child molesting Fatty "dildo man" McKellar and imprison him in the box. Like a mad scientist Ebenezer performed various experiments on the hopeless creature over a lengthy period, the first experiment involved a more financially viable alternative for castration, he proved that using a chainsaw was much more cost effective then the expensive process of chemicals, he was even nominated for a Nobel prize for his efforts in the study of how nonces can survive on a diet just rat shit and goat's piss. naturally being the generous man he is, he was able to deliver Thaddeus this specimen as a birthday present readily available for the tortures of the dammed in his new Perspex prison.

Ebenezer yanked a large iron lever and a sound similar to that of a steam train whistle emitted from the console "fuck me what does that do?" asked Thaddeus "Ebenezer laughed so hard he snorted" "just watch" he proclaimed through the laughter; Thaddeus gazed into the box as excited as a kid opening his first present on Christmas morning. Suddenly the box filled with a thick orange fog and through the mist fatty's rotting stump's could be seen thumping wildly on the glass "ha ha agent orange" exclaimed Ebenezer, "most intriguing!" replied Thaddeus "the shape of the dildo man could be faintly seen flopping around like a fish, he flopped so wildly that he managed to sever his own spinal cord, Thaddeus clapped in amusement and began to do a dance whilst singing the national anthem his arms flailing wildly, in his mad celebration he accidentally hit a large yellow button surrounded with hazard markings and labelled 'purge', "ah shit bro not that one!" yelled Ebenezer. Suddenly, the inside of the box was engulfed in flames, this time all of the soundproofing in the world wasn't enough to dull out the almighty screams the fat animal made as he was slowly burned alive "fuck!" Thaddeus yelled, "my plaything! Ebenezer quickly punched a blue button and water began to spray from nozzles in the boxes ceiling. the two men waited in anticipation as the fog and water drained, "ughh" exclaimed Ebenezer pinching his nostrils "the fucking smell, it smells like rotting roadkill" he pressed a button labelled 'extractor' and the stink quickly faded away, after a few minutes the mist finally cleared and in the corner of the tank was the incinerated pathetic body of the dildo man, his face, twisted in the most horrific pose had almost completely melted off, two deep holes remained where his eyes had popped in there sockets and his body was contorted at impossible angles as if he had been flash frozen. "kill...kill me" he begged almost incoherently "fuck me hes still alive!" Thaddeus exclaimed in joy; "brilliant" Ebenezer exclaimed high fiving his brother "shall we finish him off?" Ebenezer asked as he smiled into the soulless eye sockets of the wretched creature, thick smoke poured from his blackened mouth and through the agonising pain somewhere in his oxygen deprived brain he still clung to the thought that the brothers might have an inch of mercy and hit the incineration button again finally putting him out of his misery. Thaddeus put a

17

finger to his lips and uttered a long "hmmmm" before suddenly stating: "Nah, where's the fun in that, lets polish off another bottle and leave him until next time, besides, you need to drop your fucking hand off at the med bay before it punches a hole in the airship" "cheers to that" replied Ebenezer as he finished his glass and headed back to the table. If the fat man had any moisture whatsoever left in his body he would have cried.

CHAPTER 3: RED ALERT

Location: the "Hungry Bird" airship.

Date: June 15th, 2035

Time: 07:15hrs

Thaddeus awoke with a start, the ships arooga alarm was going off like a demonic air raid siren, "fuckinghell this is not what you need with a hangover" he thought, he rolled out of bed and slowly shuffled though the darkness toward the intercom, occasionally finding a weeks' worth of empty whiskey bottles with his feet, "Goffbot" he said weakly as he pressed the intercom buzzer "what's that fucking alarm for?", the robots voice replied almost immediately through the speaker "boss, there is an urgent message for the both of you in the control room" Thaddeus let out a loud sigh "how urgent" he replied, "boss it's from him, it's from Mr. Red" Thaddeus paused and uttered a quiet "shit" before responding: "were on our way". He pressed another button labelled E "Ebenezer are you still alive?" he asked into the intercom, a few seconds passed before Ebenezer responded "uhhhh" Ebenezer groaned through the intercom "what's that fucking din about?", "urgent message bro, we need to get to the control room", "fuck sake, on my way" Ebenezer replied, Thaddeus released his finger from the intercom button and turned to face the room "lights on" he said through a yawn before picking up his silk pink dressing gown from the floor and chucking it on, he noticed Waqa was slumped in the corner of the room completely nude but surrounded by bottles of port and partially eaten loaves of cornbread "ahh the lights man, the fucking lights" he groaned, Thaddeus turned to face the door and cleared his throat "open" he said loudly, the metal doors slid open and Thaddeus stepped into the ships corridor yelling "lights off" as he exited, wiping the sleep from his eyes he shuffled in the direction of the control room. A sudden loud crash from behind caused him to nearly jump out of his skin, he span around and watched as the door to Ebenezer's room was booted clean off and into the corridor, crushed cans of beer and empty packets of Drexel cigarettes spilled all over the place, Ebenezer slowly emerged wearing only Julius Caesars toga and what looked to be Genghis Khans war helmet. "Fucking thing malfunctioned again" he grunted as he stumbled into the corridor "Ebenezer" a female voice with an foreign accent called from his room, two prostitutes appeared from the doorway, completely nude but covered from head to toe in wholegrain mustard "come back to bed" they cooed, Ebenezer turned and grinned whilst awkwardly removing the helmet, Thaddeus laughed as he noticed he still had not picked up his new hand from the med bay, Ebenezer smiled as he adjusted his enormous mohawk "you two dont go anywhere, Il be right back" he answered in an almost psychotic voice. "And who are those two?" Thaddeus asked as the two men walked down the corridor toward the door of the control room "dont you remember?" Ebenezer replied, "we picked them up last night" "where from?" Thaddeus enquired "some bar in Moscow" Ebenezer replied with a loud yawn "ah gotcha, wait Moscow?" Thaddeus asked in a shocked voice "are you telling me were in Russia? ", "fuck me" Ebenezer said through a chuckle as the two men stopped outside the control room "maybe you should lay off the stone whiskey for a few days. Bro were about a thousand feet above St Petersburg", Thaddeus quickly looked out of the nearest porthole to be met with a view of just clouds, he suddenly vomited all over his dressing gown in what could only be described as a technicolour yawn. "impressive" Ebenezer remarked

21

before activating the control room door switch and heading inside, Thaddeus burped loudly and wiped his mouth on his sleeve before slowly following him.

"Well, what the fuck is this about?" Ebenezer boomed as he entered the control room "and can someone turn that fucking alarm off its beasting my brain" "yes boss, sorry boss" the Goffbot 4000 replied as it whirred across the steel floor on its rubber tracks, an upturned can of pringles was still wedged over its head from the last briefing. It stopped inches from the rooms control panel and inserted one of its many steel arm attachments into a circular hole silencing the alarm. Thaddeus finally staggered into the room "well go on then" he said impatiently as he leant against the wall as to not throw up again "play the fucking message". The Goffbot inserted another arm into a different shaped socket and the rooms huge display monitor suddenly came to life and the black silhouette of Mr. Red appeared, he was sat behind a walnut desk in an office somewhere and all that could be seen of him was a hand that held a cigar over a crystal ashtray, the cuff of a deep red suit just barely visible "Lord Thaddeus, Lord Ebenezer" the voice began in a masculine tone "I expect your wondering why I have summoned you and I do apologise, I know how busy you both are" Thaddeus looked down at his discoloured dressing gown and Ebenezer weakly held back a smirk as he lit a Drexel. "We currently face a serious threat" the voice continued, "our analysts here have intercepted a transmission of that of a terroristic nature, a man who only goes by the alias "The Doctor" has somehow managed to resurrect the organization known as R.I.S.E and has issued us a warning along with what he described as a small demonstration of force, I dont know quite how to tell you this fellas but the united states of America has been completely destroyed, this maniac launched some kind of energy based projectile and wiped the country from the face of the earth". "Ebenezer's mouth hung open and the cigarette fell from his lips "fuck me" Thaddeus gasped in disbelief, the message continued "the thing we can't figure out is where he launched them from, we have been scouring the earth with our satellites but to no avail, gentlemen I'm afraid that you are our last hope, if the British government is seen to mobilise troops we fear he will stay true to his word and launch another attack, we have no idea how many of these weapons he has at his disposal, we are asking you to find the R.I.S.E headquarters and terminate this madman, after which

23

destroy the source of these attacks, blow the base and get back to England in time for tea and medals. As usual you will receive payment when the task is completed and due to the highly dangerous nature of this mission the amount should be acceptable to you both, T.R.E.K.K is prepared to credit your mercenary account with ten billion credits on completion of this operation". This time it was Thaddeus's turn to drop his jaw to the ground "fuck me!" he said again "ten billion credits! bro imagine the whiskey!" he said excitedly "imagine the pussy!" Ebenezer said sharing his excitement "theres one more thing men" the voice continued "we have a lead for you, before The Doctor went offline a trace tracker was initiated in an attempt to find him, of course it was far too late to establish his location but it did pick up an electronic signature where someone else was watching the transmission, the signature was inspected and theres no doubt it came from within the Kortex HQ building in London, if I were in your position thats where I'd start, and Id begin with having a little chat with that greasy son of a bitch Mark Langley, hes the CEO. The Espartano brothers looked at each other and nodded in agreement "all thats left is for me to wish you the best of luck fellas, the safety of the world depends on you both but as always you won't receive any recognition for your work as not even the King knows about the operations of T.R.E.K.K or especially your services, but mark my words, you will each receive a medal made from solid krypton and my personal thanks.. good luck gentlemen and god speed!" the screen went black and a loud "MESSAGE TERMINATED" bellowed out of the computer, the brothers stood in silence still in shock from what they had just been told, a whole minute passed until Ebenezer finally said something "fuck the medals, fuck the thanks, ten billion credits let's get a move on!".

Thaddeus and Ebenezer wrenched the door open and ran out of the control room in the direction of the armoury "Goffbot!" Ebenezer yelled behind him "set coordinates for London and get this thing on the move!" "yes boss, roger that boss" the Goffbot whirred in response. the Russian whores peered from the door as the brothers thundered past them "shit!" Ebenezer yelled suddenly stopping and turning back to the girls "bro I'll be five minutes meet me in the armoury!" he yelled diving into the room like a mad pornstar "have a tremendous knees up, and make sure you pick up your fucking hand!" Thaddeus called after him still giddy with excitement, he turned the corner toward the armoury and suddenly a brilliant idea entered his mind, "fuck it" he said to himself changing direction to the lounge. "Alright you child molesting shit licker" he yelled as he entered the room and headed for Fatty McKellar's prison "Just in case I dont make it back, today it all ends for you, I'm putting you out of your fucking misery" the dildo mans melted face slowly turned to face his direction and Thaddeus swore he could just about make out a distorted smile of relief from the pathetic monster, the wall of death was still out from the previous week and Thaddeus marched up to it "this is it" the perverted nonce thought to himself in his deep fried brain "one more moment of pain then its finally over" Thaddeus's finger hovered over the purge button and he took one last look at Fatty's disgusting face, he watched him take his last breath then.... "actually!" Thaddeus exclaimed suddenly "like my brother said before, where's the fun in that?" laughing he hit the circular saw button and whacked the tempo dial down to the lowest setting, then with a perfectly executed about turn, he danced his way to the door leaving the dildo man to slowly but surely scream his own lungs out as he was excruciatingly vivisected by the unforgiving steel blades a millimetre at a time "see you in a week" Thaddeus called cheerfully behind him on his way out, "oops nearly forgot" he said as he leant back into the room to flip the light switch to the off position, "were quite energy efficient me and Ebenezer, anyway cheerio" the lights went out and the door slammed shut, the room was completely silent... well apart from within Fatty's prison anyway, in there it was quite the opposite.

CHAPTER 4: HOLLOW POINT.

Location: the "Hungry Bird" airship.

Date: June 15th, 2035

Time: 0745hrs

"What the fuck do R.I.S.E and T.R.E.K.K even stand for?" Ebenezer asked as he slotted a drum magazine onto Al Capones tommy gun. "fuck if I know" Thaddeus replied as he whacked a mag of AP hollow points onto the platinum AK-47 he had taken from Saddam Hussain's personal collection. A crackle suddenly came over the armoury's speaker and the Goffbot chimed in: "R.I.S.E stands for Regaining influential status across earth and T.R.E.K.K stands for Task recon kinetic knowledge. Ebenezer stopped what he was doing and looked up toward the armoury's camera "and who the fuck asked you, get back to work you mechanical asshole" the speaker quickly crackled back on "yes boss. sorry boss" Ebenezer shook his head as he stood up and examined the wall of weapons in front of him before grabbing his diamond encrusted Glock-18 custom which he span on his robotic finger "looks like Mya sorted your hand out" Thaddeus said as he watched "fuck yeah, she even added a new modification" Ebenezer replied happily "watch this!" he made a fist and as he squeezed his hand an array of gold spikes extended from his knuckles "fuckinghell! thats awesome" Thaddeus said as he walked over to check it out "yup! a solid gold knuckleduster in my own hand" Ebenezer said proudly "man I bet you dont regret catching that grenade now" Thaddeus responded "well..." Ebenezer replied "jerking off isn't exactly the same" the two men laughed and Ebenezer slid his pistol into the holster "ready to rock?" Thaddeus asked as he tossed Ebenezer a high-ex grenade, Ebenezer clicked it onto his chest rig and cracked his knuckles "let's dance" he replied with a grin and a cock of his tommy gun.

"Alright we need to check in with Core", Thaddeus announced as he stood up "he'll get us some clearance for infiltrating Kortex "fuckinghell, does he still work for us?" Ebenezer asked in a shocked tone "I haven't seen the guy in weeks", Thaddeus laughed "yeah he still works for us, but he practically lives in the server room", "well what does he eat?" Ebenezer enquired "he lives on a diet of rocket fuel and grot pots" Thaddeus answered "but if its anything to do with Intel hell get us what we need, "agreed" Ebenezer responded as the two men left the armoury and headed to the server room. Approaching the door they could hear what sounded like the world's largest tesla coil buzzing at a tremendous volume, lights flashed and danced wildly from the sides of the steel doors, Thaddeus pressed the intercom "Core? are you in there?" a short pause and a voice responded through the intercom:

"who goes there?" Core replied, "come on open up!" Thaddeus replied impatiently, suddenly there was a loud clunk and the door slowly opened, the two men stepped into the room and were shocked at what lay in front of them, the room was completely filled with computer components, not an inch of the floor was visible, there were monitors and screens affixed to every wall. and there was empty cans of rocket fuel and grot pots everywhere. In the centre of the room on top of a mountain of pizza boxes, sat Core, his face comprised of some sort of electronic visor which had been fused to his skin and his brain was exposed to allow him access to program his own neurocircuitry the two brothers had never really quite figured out what Core was but Thaddeus had a theory that he was some kind of prototype mutant cyborg sent from the future from a friendly organisation to assist the Espartano brothers in there various exploits "how's it going?" asked Ebenezer over the various blasts of static from a thousand cathode ray tube monitors "Fellas!" Core responded joyfully "how was the latest outing?". "it was a knees up thanks" Ebenezer replied, "listen Core" Thaddeus began "we need you to access the Kortex mainframe and list us as employees can you do that?", Core's visor suddenly flashed red "Root accessed, downloading data, processing...processing, access granted, you are both now clear for authorization, data has been transferred to the PDA's on the wall behind you", Thaddeus and Ebenezer exchanged an impressed look. The door swung open behind the brothers and Core stood to his feet "good luck fellas" he said executing a mock salute "thanks buddy!" Ebenezer said in a grateful tone, he grabbed a PDA from the wall and slotted it onto his arm gauntlet as he left. Thaddeus gave Core the thumbs up and did the same as his brother.

The Espartano brothers stood in the airship's enormous cargo bay either side of the landing ramp and each smoked a Drexel while they waited for the Goffbot to inform them they had arrived over the building. "Ive been thinking" Thaddeus began "I want to take point on this one bro, that son of a bitch Langley has been on my radar for some time" Ebenezer took a drag from his cigarette, "who is this fucking guy?" he asked. "hes a piece of shit who puts a price on clean air" Thaddeus replied, fury in his voice, you know how many people have died because of this mother fucker? these people go bankrupt paying for the air until finally they can't even afford to eat, they fucking starve and this son of a bitch sips whiskey in his office while he watches them do it. "Alright bro" Ebenezer said with his own trace of fury in his voice, he put his hand on Thaddeus's shoulder and asked, "how do you want to play this?" Thaddeus looked up at his brother and smiled "ok" he began "here's what were gonna fucking do..."

CHAPTER 5: KNUCKLE SANDWICH

Location: London

Date: June 15th, 2035

Time: 21:15hrs

It was the darkest night in earth's history as the airship loomed over the streets of London below and by now a deep oily blackness had completely shrouded the city. somewhere near, in a high rise building, Mark Langley: the CEO of Kortex's faint Silhouette could be seen sorting papers behind bone white blinds hiding away from public eyes, his secretary Christina was working late and she knew to her dismay that she would soon have to leave to go home, "home" she thought, as a young girl she imagined a Hollywood scene like in the old movies, she imagined the white picket fence and the kiss goodbye to her husband as he hopped in his emerald green Cadillac ready for another day at the power plant, baloney sandwiches in tow, but the cruel hand of fate had other plans for this woman, "home" was nothing but a small squalor, a rat infested shit hole and the square jawed handsome man of her dreams had been replaced by a cruel drunk of a husband who enjoyed nothing more than beating her and drinking Stella by the gallon to the point of burping the alphabet in no particular order, his favourite hobby at the moment was hurling abuse at her whilst she scrubbed the floors cleaning up the urine that he would deposit, she longed for an escape but she knew deep within her soul that she was now far far too old and hideous to ever change her situation for the better, it had seemed that fate had definitely span the wheel many times for this poor woman and with a bit of luck working as head secretary for the CEO of Kortex, her life was ruined forever, naturally she was in no rush to get home so she nervously tugged her skirt and knocked on his door "Mr Langley?" she asked quietly.

The head honcho sat back in his seat and placed his hands behind his head "let me guess, overtime" he said in a moronic tone "if... if thats ok with you?" Christina stammered. He begrudgingly agreed by a show of rolling his eyes and a deep intake of breath, "one hour" he droned on the exhale "and next time you come to work you better wear a shorter skirt" he said as he grinned like Jimmy Saville in a playground. You see the CEO is a typical corporate asswipe in nature he hates all those whom he considers "lesser mortals" he's an absolute buffoon of a man who stood at just 5 foot tall, had a top knot haircut and drove a Prius, he firmly believes that his influence over a company which regulates the supply of clean air (for a hefty price of course) was a position that demanded great respect when in actual fact he'd rob his own grandmother for her last nickel (so naturally he was already at a mental disadvantage) it was no surprise that when his secretary informed him there was a shadow that moved across the window so erratically it made her body shake with fear.. he simply passed it off and ignored the kind woman.

Thaddeus was close.

Crash! the large window to the south of the CEO's office suddenly exploded as Thaddeus ziplined through it dressed in the height of roman fashion, Christina screamed and ran out of the office as Thaddeus hit the floor and detached himself from the wire with a perfectly executed shoulder roll, he stood up and unslung his AK-47 pointing the laser sight directly at the CEO's head "who the fuck are you!" Mark Langley yelled at the armour-clad assailant, a hint of fear in his voice as he stared in horror at Thaddeus's half cyborg face, Thaddeus didn't answer, instead he lowered his aim and shot an armour piercing round directly through the little angry man's shoulder "arrgghhh!" Langley yelled in agony clutching his wound, he pushed his wheelie chair away from his desk until it backed against the wall "you mother fucker what do you want?" he bellowed in pain, again Thaddeus didn't answer instead he responded by putting another round through the other shoulder, Mark Langley let out another agonising scream as Thaddeus marched toward him throwing his desk across the room in his wake "please" the man begged, his anger turning to desperation "please no more, I'll do anything!, you want money? theres a safe, please!!" Thaddeus's laser eye shined a little brighter as he raised his assault rifle so high the barrel smashed into the ceiling panels, he brought the butt down hard into Mark Langley's face like a sledgehammer smashing his teeth out and breaking his nose "uggh!" he slurred but before he could utter another word Thaddeus brought the butt down once more, even harder this time cracking the CEO's puny skull like a fuck ugly egg and rendering him unconscious. "bro" Thaddeus said calmly into his headset "come up, hes out".

The elevator doors opened with a loud ding and the bodies of two armoured guards fell out, Ebenezer stepped out onto the top floor, blood leaked from a bullet hole in his abdomen and after holstering his meat cleaver, he stuffed the wound with gauze from his med pack, his jet and gold armour glinted in the overhead lighting as blood trickled down his breastplate, he noticed just how magnificent it looked, he lit a cigar and put another drum magazine onto his tommy gun and cocked it before heading in the direction of the CEO's office, as he walked he noticed Christina hiding behind a nearby water cooler and he stopped to look at her "working late?" he asked "I....I dont want to go home" the woman finally said shaking with fear "oh? and whys that?" Ebenezer inquired. "H-Husband" Christina gasped her voice still trembling uncontrollably, Ebenezer grunted loudly before unclipping his pistol from its holster and chambering a round, Christina closed her eyes tightly and waited for the shot, but it never came, "here" Ebenezer said shortly handing her his Glock "wha-whats this for?" Christina asked in a shocked tone, Ebenezer smiled "you want to live in fear forever?" he said firmly before turning and walking away. Christina looked at the handgun she held in her palms and slowly she began to feel something inside of her she hadn't felt in years, a sensation she wasn't sure if she would ever feel again, power. she put the Glock into her handbag, got up and walked to the elevator stepping over the dead men as she did so, as the doors began to close Ebenezer turned and looked at her, she smiled gratefully, he nodded in response.

"You son of a bitch give me a fucking name!" Thaddeus yelled into Langley's face, "uggh, uhhh" the Man groaned pathetically struggling against his restraints, Ebenezer entered the room and saw that Thaddeus had secured the CEO into his wheelie chair with razor wire so tightly that it had cut into his flesh "good job bro!" Ebenezer exclaimed slapping Thaddeus a high five, "yeah we got this son of a bitch good" Thaddeus replied wiping blood from the organic side of his face "you ok?" he asked noticing Ebenezer's bullet wound "it's nothing, went in and out" Ebenezer replied reassuringly, he strode up to Langley and delivered a knuckle sandwich into his terrified grid with his new fist augmentation knocking him and the chair off the ground, it crashed back down onto the floor and Langley let out a half unconscious groan, Ebenezer reached down and grabbed the CEO by his top knot with his powerful cybernetic fist "fucking wake up!" he bellowed lifting the man off the floor, chair and all. "if I tell you I'm a dead man" Langley managed to splutter, broken teeth falling from his mouth "your fucking dead anyway! last chance asshole!" Thaddeus said impatiently as he joined his brother in the interrogation "right I dont have time for this" Ebenezer roared as he unsheathed his machete from its holster "fucking speak up or prepare to taste cold steel!", the CEO let out a small chuckle "I-I know what that means" he squeaked still in the grasp of Ebenezer's fist "once you take them out you have to kill with them, so why should I bother spilling my guts if I'm already dead?" he spat with a hint of a sneer, Ebenezer looked at Thaddeus and laughed "looks like this assholes done his research" "correct!!" he yelled into Langley's eardrum which burst instantly, "we always kill when we take them out fucker, but what your missing is how long we take doing it, and as for spilling your guts, well.." with that Ebenezer shoved the enormous blade all the way through the man's stomach until it burst through the back of the chair, Langley let out a bloodcurdling scream, his face reflected his agony as Ebenezer lifted him and the wheelie chair completely off the floor with the machete and walked toward the open window, guts and stomach acid spilled all over his gorgeous armour as he strode, Thaddeus cheered as he walked behind, "give..me..a..name!!" Ebenezer yelled at the helpless man as he held him at the windows edge, Mark Langley could no longer string an intelligible sentence together but just managed to point at his upturned desk, "draw", he spluttered amidst a death rattle spraying blood into Ebenezer's face "thank you" Ebenezer replied sarcastically before unclipping a high ex grenade from his belt, "enjoy your trip" he pulled the pin and stuffed the grenade down the CEO's gullet so hard he swallowed his own Adams apple, then with an almighty boot he kicked Langley clean off the blade and out of the window where he fell silently gurgling to his death.

"Fuck!" Ebenezer exclaimed with a laugh looking at his machete "bro look at this!" Thaddeus who had made his way to the desk turned and looked at what Ebenezer had found, "fuck me!" Thaddeus said in an impressed voice, Mark Langley's ribcage swung from the blade of the espartano machete "gotta love these things" Ebenezer said as he removed the ribcage and booted it out of the window.

"Bro, come and look at this" Thaddeus said suddenly in a shocked tone, Ebenezer walked over and looked at what Thaddeus had taken from the CEO's draw, suddenly a loud bang could be heard from outside and Ebenezer smiled to himself before taking the object Thaddeus handed to him, he identified the object as what appeared to be a solid gold skull "the fuck is this?" he asked "take a look at the engraving" Thaddeus replied, Ebenezer turned the item over and read the inscription on the underside "FTOOTD" he spelled out loud.

Thaddeus and Ebenezer looked at each other in silence... "from the office of the dean" Thaddeus said in a shocked tone.

"Goffbot, fire up the turbines were coming back aboard" Ebenezer barked into his headset.

"uhh ok boss" the robot pilot whirred back "where too boss?"

Ebenezer looked at Thaddeus and they both nodded in agreement.

"were going to Oxford, tell core we need some more clearance and get that fucking armoury open were gonna need to bring out the big guns."

CHAPTER 6: ENTER THE DEAN.

Location: Oxford University

Date: June 16th, 2035

Time: 0800hrs

"**F**uck me, his drinks globe is even more fancy then the one back in the airship" Ebenezer exclaimed whilst gently whirling the solid gold globe around on its chrome axis, the office door creaked open and a short fat woman with horn rimmed glasses appeared "the dean will be with you shortly gentlemen, he asked for you to help yourself to a drink from the globe or a cigar from his humidor", "Thanks, we will indeed, now off you go" Ebenezer replied flatly. The fat woman tutted and left the two men to indulge" I can't believe these passes worked so well" Thaddeus exclaimed admiring the shopped image on his PDA, "Core's outdone himself this time" he jumped off the leather armchair and headed for the davenport "dont mind if I do" he exclaimed gleefully as he flung open the lid of the cedar box, "wow!" Thaddeus remarked as he sniffed one of Castro's personal Cubans "impeccable taste in cigars" Ebenezer smiled "and cognac" he added helping himself to a bottle from the globe "what a man" he added, Thaddeus agreed "it almost seems a shame to put a bullet in his fucking head" he laughed whilst shoving a handful of cigars into his waistcoat, Ebenezer sat on the deans throne and put his feet up on the marble desk "look at all those" he said in admiration gesturing with his glass to the row of family crests that hung on the wall of the office "impressive!" Thaddeus agreed "but not as impressive as ours" it was a true statement indeed, back in the airship there was a spectacular coat of arms hung in the lounge, the shield itself was hand crafted by Waqa Waqa, it was forged from the bonnet of Adolf Hitlers Mercedes Benz and the weapons mounted behind it were none other than enormous machetes of the highest degree, the blades themselves were made of solid tungsten and the handles were fashioned from the door knockers of Windsor castle itself.

The door behind them suddenly opened once more and in the doorway stood the most marvellous looking son of a bitch the brothers had ever laid eyes on, he was tall, with a pinstripe valentino suit and Italian leather shoes, his watch was a band of wafer-thin solid gold and his tie looked as though it had been purchased

43

from the house of Fraser's winter collection. "gentlemen" he voice cooed smoothly "I am the dean of oxford university, and in contrast to what your ID's say I'm guessing you are the Espartano Brothers?" he said smugly, "I have been expecting you, now how may I be of assistance?" "please" Ebenezer replied removing himself from the dean's throne "sit down, we have a couple of questions for you". "I have nothing to hide" the dean replied sitting in his throne and pushing back his chestnut brown hair, "maybe you can explain this" Thaddeus said flatly, unzipping his Kevlar vest, he pulled out the golden skull and walloped it down on the dean's desk so hard it almost cracked the gorgeous marble finish "start talking you smooth prick" he said angrily. the dean put his feet up on the desk and crossed his legs, lighting a cigar he began to talk.

"A few months ago myself and a small number of other carefully selected people received a telegram from a man who only identified himself as "The Doctor", the telegram outlined a plan to essentially govern the world, it identified certain company's with the resources to make this an achievable goal, the telegram went on to explain that "The Doctor" had the funding and the inspiration to change mankind forever, and that if I were

44

to join this man's organisation I would have unlimited power at my disposal"

"I think we can safely assume that Mark Langley was a name on that list?" Ebenezer asked.

The dean cleared his throat and re-adjusted himself in his chair "I did read about his misfortune, or should I say your good fortune in dispatching him".

"Quite" Thaddeus replied his hand tapping the walnut handle of his machete.

"As I was saying" the dean continued "he wanted me to work alongside him in his organisation, he recognised that I could influence the great minds within this university to pledge their allegiance to him, he said that we could do amazing things together and change the course of history in the process".

"So thats why he wanted Langley" Thaddeus remarked leaning forward in his chair "because he controlled the air supply".

The dean slowly stood up and put his fists on his desk "makes you think who else could be on his list doesn't it Gentlemen?"

Ebenezer jumped to his feet and raised his tommy gun "well were going to find out, aren't we?"

The dean bowed his head and to the brothers surprise he started laughing "what's so fucking funny?" Thaddeus demanded unslinging his AK-47 and cocking the handle. "you fools" The dean said in a malicious tone "you seem to have it confused, I'm not the one in trouble here, you are" he quickly hit a hidden button built into the desks surface and a transparent box whooshed down from a recess in the celling surrounding him and his desk. Thaddeus and Ebenezer lifted there firearms and let rip the entire contents of each magazine into the box, not a scratch, then, through speakers hidden in the room the dean announced to the brothers "bulletproof gentlemen, just like how most people think you are, perhaps now would be a good time to test that theory, now if you dont mind, I have somewhere to be, good luck" the dean hit another button and with a whirr the entire box lowered into the floor until it had disappeared entirely, in its place was nothing more than a square of titanium. "son of a bitch!" Ebenezer roared. Suddenly from the corridor the sounds of boots could be heard running toward the office "fuck, bro get ready!" Thaddeus yelled quickly changing the magazine on his

AK "were giving you ten seconds to come out with your hands on your head or were coming in" a voice from behind the door suddenly boomed, the mechanical clicks of assault rifles cocking could be heard followed by an authority filled voice "Ten" it yelled "fuck theres gotta be a whole squad out there!" Ebenezer said taking aim at the door "no fucking surrender bro" Thaddeus exclaimed "were fighting our way out of here" Thaddeus marched to the office window, peering into the campus courtyard he could see a squad of the dean's henchmen jumping out of an armoured land rover and forming into a tactical column "ah shit theres more of them!" he yelled "we need to move now!" "Nine" the voice yelled again from behind the door "fuck you!" Ebenezer yelled back, from his back sheath he pulled an enormous boomstick and with an ear-piercing bang he blew the solid oak door completely off its hinges into the corridor behind it, "go! go!" a voice could be heard through the smoke before a handful of guards clad in what looked to be surplus SWAT gear seeped into the room. Thaddeus raised his AK and fired wildly into the group, the first few rounds hit the front man in the head and neck, blood sprayed across the office and with a loud gurgle he fell to his knees, the group returned fire at Thaddeus but there bullets bounced off his golden armour, Ebenezer drew his espartano machete and leapt into the crowd, he let out a fearsome war cry as he sliced and diced the assailants, blood and chunks of flesh flew all over the place until only one man remained, he had a gunshot wound to his stomach and writhed around on the floor in agony groaning loudly as he did so, Ebenezer stamped on his wound with his enormous boot and the fucker screamed in agony "where is he you son of a bitch! where did the dean go!?" the henchmen continued to scream blue murder, his pathetic attempts to remove the boot from his gut useless. "I said where did he fucking go!" Ebenezer yelled applying more pressure, again there was nothing but screams "ah fuck this" Thaddeus said loudly "let's have a blast with that" he said pointing at Ebenezer's boomstick, Ebenezer handed the beautiful weapon to Thaddeus with delight "very nice" Thaddeus remarked examining the patterns of gold inlay that delicately swept through the gun's woodwork. His admiration of the firearm was interrupted by the ever loud screaming of the pathetic man, Thaddeus shoved the boomstick into the poor fucker's eye socket and blew his brains all over the wall behind him.

CHAPTER 7: ROAD-RASH.

Location: Oxford University Campus

Date: June 16th, 2035

Time: 08:30hrs

The Zephyr's tyres screeched as Thaddeus slammed on the gas, a hail of bullets bounced off the back of the car and Ebenezer returned fire as he leant rearwards from the passenger window "eat shit you mother fuckers!" he yelled as he pumped round after round into the armoured land rover tailgating behind them. "fuck even the AP rounds wont punch it" he yelled over the gunfire, Thaddeus was driving like a man possessed, "the boot!" he yelled to Ebenezer as he swerved the car manically around the campus grounds "in the boot bro!" Ebenezer tucked back inside the car just in time as the wingmirror was shot to bits in front of him, he dived into the back of the car and ripped the rear seat out, "get down!" Thaddeus yelled as bullets ripped through the rear window "fuck!" he cursed, taking a sudden left turn out of the courtyards and onto the university's exit road, he adjusted the rear-view mirror and watched as the land rover followed in the same path "were sitting ducks!" he called back to Ebenezer, "not for long" Ebenezer replied excitedly Thaddeus turned and saw Ebenezer had pulled the Vulcan minigun from the boot "Ok bro here's the plan!" Thaddeus said quickly reaching for a red button on the dash.

"Come on take these fuckers off the road!" Captain Jackson yelled to his men as he rammed the back of the Zephyr with his armoured land rover "we take these two pricks out and the dean with reward us handsomely" he laughed as he rammed the car again, smashing the rear taillights, his men shooting furiously from the windows with SMG's. Suddenly the Zephyr took off at a tremendous speed, the gap grew further and further away from the land rover "son of a bitch!" Captain Jackson yelled "they're getting away!" try as he might the land rover couldn't keep up, then, completely without warning the car suddenly skidded sideways and came to a halt in the middle of the road "now Ive fucking got you!" Jackson said triumphantly as he headed on a direct collision course with the sideways Zephyr, suddenly his victory was cut short as he watched the hulking figure of Ebenezer exit the vehicle and point his enormous minigun directly at him "no!" he screamed as bullets ripped through the engine block and armoured windshield, hitting him in the shoulder and chest Captain Jackson screamed in pain as he tried hopelessly to control the vehicle.

From the driver's seat of the Zephyr Thaddeus watched in total enjoyment as his brother slowly walked toward the oncoming vehicle unleashing a seemingly unlimited amount of bullets from his minigun, Ebenezer threw his head back in laughter as the land rover lost control and flipped sideways, it span two or three times in the air before finally coming to a crashing halt drivers side down on the tarmac just meters from where Ebenezer stood, he released his finger from the miniguns trigger and after the sounds of bullet casings pinging off the ground stopped, all was quiet. Thaddeus pulled his AK-47 from the driver's door rack and left the car to join his brother. suddenly the land rover's passenger door creaked open and Captain Jackson desperately pulled himself from the wreckage. Ebenezer chuckled to himself as Jackson rolled from the vehicle and landed on his back on the tarmac he coughed and spluttered, blood jetting from his mouth as he did so. Ebenezer pulled a cigar from his pocket and lit it before walking slowly toward the captain, the minigun still slung to his side.

Thaddeus checked over the vehicle as his brother began to "question" the wounded commander "all clear" Thaddeus yelled to Ebenezer as he blasted the last surviving henchman directly in his cerebral cortex, he looked upon the shredded remains of the land rovers' inhabitants and noticed a laptop on the footwell of the driver's seat, "hmm" he muttered before grabbing it "worth a look", he took the laptop and flung it into the back seat of the Zephyr. "well how do you want it?" Ebenezer asked patiently as he stood above the injured man "fuck you!" Jackson spat in response as he writhed in his own blood "ok" Ebenezer said as he slowly unsheathed his Espartano machete, a grin spreading from ear to ear "slowly it is".

With a loud crash the zephyr smashed through the solid iron gates of the university and headed to the airship, Ebenezer turned in his seat and looked out of the rear window, his face held host to the biggest beaming smile Thaddeus had seen to date "how long do you think hell last?" Thaddeus asked "if we keep it under sixty I reckon hell make it to the airship" Ebenezer laughed in response, Thaddeus adjusted the rear-view mirror and could see the scalped body of Captain Jackson as he was dragged from the rear bumper, face down his hands tied behind his back the two brothers could just make out his agonising screams as his face was tore to the bone from road rash. "what's with the laptop?" Ebenezer said as he pulled it from the back seat, "Intel" Thaddeus answered as he lit a Drexel "well give it to Core when we get back, if anyone can get anything out of it its him", Ebenezer nodded in agreement before lobbing the laptop over his shoulder back into the car's rear.

The Zephyr finally entered the industrial estate where the airship was docked and Ebenezer got on the comms "Goffbot, lower the ramp were coming aboard" a few seconds passed before he spoke again "Goffbot! I said lower the ramp you useless fucking moron" finally a deranged voice crackled in response through the speakers "so the espartano brothers have forgotten there keys huh? well this airships mine fuckers!" the voice yelled, "shit" Thaddeus cursed pounding his fist into the dashboard "who the fuck is that?", "I hope you dont mind I take her for a spin" the voice continued with a laugh "the dean told me that if me and my lads delivered it to him then I'll get a seat in the organisation". "Alright" Ebenezer said "well bite, who the fuck are you?" there was a pause then the voice spoke again, slower and more seriously this time "this is Jimmy Whizz, and if you know that name you know to back the fuck off!" the communication cut off and Ebenezer exhaled loudly "well?" he asked after a short pause, "any idea who the fuck he is?" Thaddeus shook his head as he typed data into his PDA, slowly he looked back at Ebenezer and Ebenezer could see he had a look in his eye that would make even the devil himself shake with fear, "I'll tell you who he is" Thaddeus said, his voice trembling with rage "hes a fucking dead man, that son of a bitch controls the distribution of Zial, hes the leader of street thunder, a rag tag bunch of war criminals" he turned and kicked the door of the Zephyr clean off and got out of the car, Ebenezer grabbed the laptop from the back seat and did the same as his brother, door and all. "We'll take the emergency entrance, how are you for ammo?", "shit! I'm empty" Thaddeus replied as he released the magazine from his AK "well, it looks like were going in the old-fashioned way" Ebenezer replied as he kicked off Captain Jacksons fleshless skull "winner!" he bellowed as it landed in an oil drum with a satisfying splat. he threw the empty minigun into a nearby skip and unsheathed his Espartano, Thaddeus drew his own blade and together they strode toward the Hungry Bird. "this is our fucking airship" Ebenezer said full of anger as he tossed a grenade over his shoulder into the driver's seat of the Zephyr "nobody's getting their hands on that, now let's paint the walls red".

CHAPTER 8: CHIN FIRST, PAIN SECOND.

Location: the "Hungry Bird" airship.

Date: June 16th, 2035

Time: 09:50hrs

Thaddeus and Ebenezer crept slowly under the belly of the airship until around the halfway point where they crouched under the access hatch Waqa had installed for scenarios just like this, Thaddeus reached up and removed the cover from a small access panel to reveal a fingerprint scanner, he held up this thumb to the scanner and the hatch silently slid open "alright, lets fucking do this" he whispered to Ebenezer before slowly peering his head through the hatch. In the dimly lit garage Thaddeus could just make out two figures who stood at the entrance to the deck lift, one of them had a green mullet and had his hands in his pockets whilst smoking. The other was completely bald and was spray painting something on the garage wall, Thaddeus held back a snigger "bro look at these clowns" he said through a grin, Ebenezer's mohawked head slowly appeared next to Thaddeus's and he looked in the direction of his brothers gaze "fuck me!" he whispered "they look like something out of a zombie apocalypse movie, look at their spikey baseball bats and those punk boots" he quietly sniggered "Oi!" the mullet punk suddenly yelled at the other, his voice echoing through the garage, "stop pissin about and get your arse back into position, Jimmy will lose his fuckin nut if he catches you, those two mother fuckers are out there you know?", "so!" the bald punk said obnoxiously as he chucked the spray can across the cargo bay, "it's not like hes paying us fuck all is it?, and those two arseholes can't get in anyway, the fucking doors welded!", "think of the fuckin zial man" the mullet punk said as he grabbed him by the arms "Jimmy's fucking connected man, hell set us up for life!". "Right let's waste these fuckers!" Thaddeus said as he reached through the access panel and placed the laptop on the floor, slowly he hoisted himself through the panel and picked up the laptop, silently he crept into the shadows of the cargo bay and ducked behind a large stack of used tyres, Ebenezer grinned to himself and followed taking a position next to Thaddeus "right well leave his here and grab it later" Thaddeus said as he hid the laptop in a gap in the tyres, slowly he unsheathed his machete, "let's take it slow and try to keep the element of surprise, no sudden movements or noise" just as he finished his sentence he saw the bald punk pick up a bottle from the floor and begin to yank on its cork "son of a bitch!" Thaddeus whispered in anger "what?" Ebenezer whispered back "what is it?" "thats my fucking whiskey!" Thaddeus said full of rage "that bottle is nearly 100 years old, it was fucking given to me personally by Winston Churchill and that piece of shit is about to chug it!" Suddenly Thaddeus snapped, he leapt from the shadows and with a loud roar he charged at the two men who stood frozen in complete terror "you mother fuckers!" he yelled as he rammed his machete through both men like a kebab skewer and pinned them to the cargo bay wall, the punks let out a simultaneous scream of pain and the bottle was sent flying, Ebenezer ran from his hiding spot and dived through the air just in time to catch it in his arms like he would if it were a new born baby. "got it!" he yelled triumphantly as he stood to his feet admiring the bottle. Thaddeus had the bald punk by the throat as he gazed deep into his soul "going to drink my fucking whiskey?" he bellowed into the man's face, the punk stuck his tongue out and spat blood into Thaddeus's face "fuck off!" he yelled painfully, "oh you want to play huh?" Thaddeus responded "ok, let's play" he grabbed the sides of the punks head and engaged his cybernetic laser eye "huhhhhh, ahhhhhhh!!!!" the punk screamed as the laser slowly burned through his forehead "fuckkk!!" he screamed through gritted teeth his eyes wide with terror as the laser cut through his skull and into his brains frontal lobe, the screaming increased and the punk kicked his legs wildly beneath him, the movement causing the laser to dance around his brain at random angles, chunks of grey matter slid from his dome and fell to the floor, the mullet punk impaled behind him had pissed himself in terror and now began to scream for help, Ebenezer laughed as he joined his brother to watch the spectacle "somehow I dont even think a lobotomy could make this guy any thicker bro" he laughed slapping Thaddeus on the shoulder, the bald punk finally fell silent as the laser burned all the way through the back of his head which now split in two like a watermelon. Ebenezer clapped with joy as he approached the second man "fuck me!" he said to the mullet punk "how am I gonna beat that?" the punk gulped and quivered in fear.

Another group of punks occupied the elevators entrance to the upper deck, beer cans littered the hallway and most of the men were passed out on the floor but one that was still standing would occasionally belch or smash a beer can against his forehead before throwing it at the Goffbot 4000 which had been spray painted multiple colours and duct taped to the ceiling, it whirred helplessly as another can bashed into its metal torso "haaaaa!" the leather jacket clad punk who threw the can yelled triumphantly as he stuck his tongue out at the others. "hey Warhawk, your turn!" a voice called from Ebenezer's room, a greasy bearded half naked punk stepped out from the doorway and zipped up his fly as he walked to the others, "he stopped before passing the leather jacket punk and smiled "I hope you like sloppy seconds Warhawk" he laughed before elbowing past him, "hey fuck you Nightrider!" Warhawk called after him, he swigged another beer as he staggered toward Ebenezer's room "well well" he said as he looked inside "what have we here?" the two beaten Russian prostitutes whimpered with fear as Warhawk began to unzip his leather chaps.

"hey, get the fuck out here!" nightrider slurred "what...! what the fuck is it, I'm busy" Warhawk yelled in response "the elevator!" nightrider called "it's coming up!" Warhawk shook his head "it's probably just that asshole Ridgeback wanting a refill, now fuck off I'm busy with the ladies" he yelled back as he activated a boombox, which blared Skrewdriver at max volume. Nightrider swigged a beer and watched as the elevator slowly came to a stop in front of him, the doors whizzed open and dropping the beer can he screamed at the sight before him, Ebenezer stomped out of the elevator, his espartano dripping blood everywhere, he entire body was splattered in claret and through the eyeholes of ridgebacks face he let out an evil growl "like my new mullet?" he asked as he advanced on nighthawk "uh...uh!" nighthawk stuttered as he stepped backwards tripping over beer cans and falling on his ass. Thaddeus now emerged from the elevator swinging a spiked baseball bat whilst whistling "shell be coming round the mountain", with a sickening crack he smashed the bat into one of the passed-out punks faces and yanked it back out of his skull by using his boot as a lever. Ebenezer heard the screams of the two women from his bedroom and he immediately saw red, to nightriders horror he slowly peeled ridgebacks face from his own and threw it against one of the corridors steel walls where it stuck with a splat and slowly starting sliding down the wall, then with one swift movement he thrust his machete into nighthawks chest and stamped on the fat fuckers throat before he could make a sound, "drink my beer and fuck my whores!?" he yelled, there was a loud "crack!" as Ebenezer crushed his windpipe and nighthawk writhed around in agonising pain as he desperately tried to take in air, Thaddeus was busy dispatching the remaining punks with the bat and his emachete, still whistling away as he did so, Ebenezer knelt on nighthawks chest and thrust two mechanical fingers into each of his eye sockets, Nighthawk gurgled loudly as Ebenezer gripped the inside of his skull like a bowling bowl and tore his viscerocranium completely off, he stood up leaving the punk to slowly choke to death on his own blood and made his way to his bedroom. "Thaddeus, check the other rooms" he called back to his brother who had just finished scalping the last of the punks "roger!" Thaddeus replied with a smile.

Behind you! one of the Russian prostitutes yelled as Ebenezer stormed into his bedroom, from behind the door Warhawk wearing only his grotty Y-fronts leapt onto Ebenezer's back, stabbing wildly into his shoulder with a push dagger, "argh you mother fucker" Ebenezer roared as he threw Warhawk over his shoulder, he landed on the bed with the hookers, the push knife leaving his hands and flying across the room "grab that piece of shit!" Ebenezer yelled to the girls, they grabbed him by each arm and held him onto the bed "let go you fucking skanks, ill fucking skin you both alive!" Warhawk screamed in anger, Ebenezer marched over and grabbed Warhawk by his ponytail lifting him up to the ceiling, "another fucking rapist huh? dont you have any fucking spine?" he rammed his mechanical hand through Warhawks stomach and grabbed hold of his spinal cord" oh there it is" Ebenezer chuckled loudly, the punks eyeballs rolled back into his head and he let out a shrill shriek which was cut short as Ebenezer swiftly ripped the upper half of his skeleton out of his body, the girls screams quickly turned to cheers as Ebenezer held half a skeleton in one hand and an empty bag of punk skin in the other "fucking shitheel" he scoffed as he threw the twitching remains into the corner of the room.

"It's clear" Thaddeus gasped as he leant into the bedroom doorway, his face dripping blood from a deep laceration "looks like Goffbot managed to seal all of the doors before they got to him, Core, Waqa and Mya are all holed up in the med bay, there was a couple of them outside trying to get in but I fucked them up, one of the mother fuckers slashed me with a cut throat" Ebenezer groaned "yeah this mother fucker got me too" he replied as he held his shoulder which now oozed blood "fuck!" Thaddeus yelled as he helped put pressure on the wound "you ok?" he asked worryingly "I'm fine" Ebenezer replied, "the fucking airships taking off, that asshole Jimmy must have figured out the controls, we need to get to the bridge!", "alright" Thaddeus replied "let's move!"

CHAPTER 9: WHIZZING JIMMY.

Location: the "Hungry Bird" airship.

Date: June 16th, 2035

Time: 10:15 hrs

The two brothers thundered down the hallway toward the control room, the Goffbot whirred helplessly from the ceiling above as they passed under it "stop fucking winging, we'll be back for in a minute" Ebenezer yelled over his shoulder as he reached the control room door, "right you scumbag piece of shit!, open this fucking door so we can rip you to pieces like we did your men" Ebenezer said angrily into the intercom "as you wish" the voice sneered back though the speaker. To the brothers surprise the doors to the control room slid open and there at the airships controls stood the wretched figure of Jimmy Whizz, he was around 6 foot tall with spiky bleach blonde hair and over his shoulders hung a dirty brown trench coat which finished at his ruined converse all-stars, the trench coat encased a dirty ill-fitting suit which he opened one side of the jacket to reveal a large supply of zial inhaler's "fancy a hit?" he asked in a crackly voice as he brought one to his lips.

"Listen here you fucking shithead!" Ebenezer bellowed as he stepped forward towards Jimmy, "I don't know who the fuck you think you are but we're not just going to let a few grotty men help themselves to our ship, now get away from those controls before I take your fucking head off", Jimmy Whizz tutted loudly and shook his head as zial vapour left his mouth "Id step back if I were you" he warned sternly has he pulled a small detonator from his trench coat pocket "this is a deadman's switch" he said as he armed the detonator with a beep and waved it at the brothers. "This whole room is wired, my hand comes off this switch and kaboom, bye bye airship, now you two are going to turn around and get off this ship, Ive got a schedule to keep" Thaddeus laughed and raised his machete in Jimmy's direction, "are you fucking deaf?, didn't you hear what I said? my hand comes of this switch and we all fucking die!", Jimmy yelled in a condescending tone, "well" Thaddeus chuckled "we better make sure it stays on there then" suddenly he launched his machete with incredible force sending it whooshing through the air and slicing Jimmy's hand clean off at the wrist "ahhhhhh!! mother fucker!" Jimmy screamed as he clutched his arm and fell to his knees, the detonator landed on the floor in front of Ebenezer, the hand still firmly gripping the trigger" fucking winner!" Ebenezer yelled as he punched his fist to the sky "hell of a shot bro!" he congratulated Thaddeus as he picked up the hand, Thaddeus marched over toward Jimmy who was writhing painfully in his own blood which sprayed from his wrist like a fountain, "come here you little shit" Thaddeus growled as he grabbed Jimmy by the throat. "fuck you!" Jimmy rasped as he squirmed frantically in Thaddeus's grip, Ebenezer strode over and unsheathed his meat cleaver "look into Thaddeus's eyes!" he bellowed "I said look in his fucking eyes, harder! harder still you mother fucker!!" Jimmy complied "thats better!" Ebenezer yelled before slamming his cleaver into the elbow of Jimmy's functional arm, Jimmy let out another blood curdling scream and waved his partly amputated limbs around wildly spraying blood all over the brothers, Thaddeus licked the blood from around his mouth and squeezed Jimmy's throat even tighter "hang in their mate, nearly done" Ebenezer laughed as he bent down and grabbed Jimmy's ankle, "fuck sake!" Ebenezer said over the screams whilst inspecting his cleaver "fucking things getting blunt, sorry Jimmy this might take a few tries, over and over again he smashed the meat cleavers dull blade into Jimmy's legs each time Jimmy's screams becoming louder and louder "nearly there!" he said over Jimmy's pitiful wails, finally he stood up and took a step back to admire the spectacle, Jimmy gurgled blood as his limbless torso hung under Thaddeus's grip "oops almost forgot" Ebenezer exclaimed as he reached over and swiftly ripped Jimmy's penis off his body with his mechanical hand and rammed it down his throat "Thats better!" Thaddeus responded in approval "nice and quiet now" Jimmy's eyes rolled back in his head and only the most wretched of sounds could be heard escaping from his airway "hey bro Ive got a sweet idea" Thaddeus said suddenly "open the window, quick before this fucker dies on us!" "uhh sure thing bro" Ebenezer replied as he walked to the window "it's gonna be pretty noisy were about 800ft in the air" Ebenezer wrenched the window open and a huge blast of air accompanied by a loud whistle emitted from the opening, Thaddeus slowly strode his way to Ebenezer and stuffed Jimmy out of the window still clutching his throat "I think it's time you got off" he said with a sickening grin "so long asshole!" Ebenezer yelled as Thaddeus let go of his throat.

Suddenly there was an enormous bang, and the two brothers were sent flying across the room into the opposite wall, the goffbot 4000 suddenly flew through the doors and crashed into the control panel "fuck!!" Thaddeus yelled "what the fuck was that" "WARNING!" a loud alarm came across the control rooms speakers "TURBINE 2 MALFUNCTION!" "shit!" Ebenezer yelled to Thaddeus "bro you threw him into the fucking engine" Thaddeus could see his brother was holding back a grin even with the impending doom at hand "Goffbot!" Thaddeus yelled as the airship began its downward spiral toward earth "get control of this ship you useless piece of shit!" the Goffbot whirred frantically as it stabbed its various arm attachments at the control panel beneath it "600 FEET!" the computerised voice blared through the speakers "Goffbot send an alert through all areas of the airship for personnel to brace for impact!" Ebenezer bellowed "400 FEET!" the voice boomed again "Goffbot get control for fucks sake" Thaddeus yelled as he adapted the brace position "uhhh I think ive got it boss" the Goffbot responded "REVERSE THRUST ENGAGED" the voice alerted as the airship gradually began to slow its descent, "were still coming in too fast!" Thaddeus yelled over the racket of the engine "200 feet!" the voice thundered once again through the speakers "bro!" Ebenezer yelled to his brother offering his hand "it's been a fucking pleasure!" Thaddeus gripped his brothers' hand in return "see you on the other side!" he yelled in reply. "IMPACT IMMINENT" Thaddeus and Ebenezer shut their eyes.

CHAPTER 10: ICARUS.

Location: London

Date: June 16th, 2035

Time: 10:30 hrs

Laura Cairney rested her head on her husband's shoulder as they admired the house in front of them "oh Paul" she said happily "I can't believe it's finally finished, it looks even nicer then before" Paul Cairney smiled to himself proudly, day and night he had put in the back-breaking hours of work slowly getting the dilapidated house back to a standard where his family could finally get off the streets and move back in, the amount of time and effort he had put in since some hooligan knocked half his house down and set it on fire was truly a marvel. "phew!" he gasped wiping his sweat sodden brow "all week, day and night" he said proudly as he admired his house "kids!" Laura called down the street "leave that ball alone and come and see what your father has done".

Jamie put the ball down and took his sister by the arm "c'mon!" he said excitedly as they ran toward the house "no more nights on the street for us, dads fixed the house!" Laura embraced the children as Paul stood in front of them his back to the house "well? What are you waiting for?" he grinned "last one to the front door is a rotten…" "Paul!" Laura interrupted "what's that?" she pointed toward the sky behind him "what?" Paul replied impatiently, he turned around watched in complete horror as the Hungry Bird airship hurtled toward them like an intercontinental ballistic missile. "fuckinghell!" Paul yelled "Run!!", the family turned and ran as fast as they could toward a nearby alleyway, just as they made it inside Paul turned and watched in complete devastation as the airship smashed directly into his newly repaired house with an enormous crash, bricks and debris were thrown everywhere and a huge cloud of dust blasted skyward, Paul and Laura huddled with the children on the alleys floor and waited for the wreckage to stop flying.

Finally, after what seemed like hours the carnage had subsided, Paul poked his head up and squinted through the dust at the enormous airship which now rested where his house would have been "mother fucker!" he spluttered through a cough, he got up and slowly walked though the rubble toward the ship waving the dust from in front of him as he went. Suddenly with a loud bang a panel was ejected from the side of the airship and landed on the street with a crash. He watched as the ship's robot the Goffbot 4000 was booted through the hatch and flew screaming across the street where it smashed to bits into a nearby bus shelter "fucking useless cunt!" Ebenezer yelled as he leapt from the escape hatch, Thaddeus jumped down after him holding his bloodied head "fuck that hurt!" he said loudly before lighting a Drexel, Thaddeus grinned as he watched, "you alright?" he asked Ebenezer "no!" he said angrily "I'm not fucking alright, that useless robot let the airship get taken, then he fucking crashed it and above all else my sunglasses were in my pocket and when the ship crashed, they fucking broke!" he pulled the two halves of his ray ban wayfarers out of his pocket and crushed them in his enormous hand. "umm excuse me?" Paul asked nervously as he slowly approached the two men "that was my house you landed on and now we don't have anywhere to live!" Ebenezer stared at the man with look on his face like he wanted to ram his fist into his stomach. "you think I fucking give a shit!?" he yelled as he grabbed Paul by the collar and lifted him off the ground "please!" Laura called from the alleyways entrance still hugging the two children, Ebenezer let go and Paul fell to the ground coughing as he caught his breath "That's better" Ebenezer said as he dusted his hands "manners cost noting" Thaddeus reached into his waistcoat pocket and pulled out the golden skull he had nabbed from Mark Langley "here" he said as he tossed it to Paul Cairney "that should be worth a few credits" Paul caught the skull and he gazed at it wide eyed in disbelief "oh my god!" he said excitedly as he scrambled to his feet "Laura, Laura look!" he held up the skull and she put her hand over her mouth in shock "we can buy a mansion with this; how can I ever repay you?" Ebenezer smiled as he put a Drexel to his lips "got a light?" he asked in reply, "Ive fucking lost mine".

The Espertano brothers clambered back aboard the airship as Ebenezer dragged the Goffbot behind him, Thaddeus hit the corridors intercom switch, "Waqa, Core, Mya" he asked "everyone ok?" a few seconds passed then a voice buzzed back through the speaker "shit, ah think ahm gonna need some port after that ordeal my brothers" the voice of Waqa responded "were all ok in here, just a little shook up is all" Thaddeus grinned to Ebenezer "Waqa well meet you all in the cargo bay in 10 it looks like we've got some work to do" he released his finger from the intercom and turned to face Ebenezer "you better check on your bitches I'll make sure McKellar survived, if hes fucking dead then this truly is the worst day of my life", "agreed" Ebenezer replied as they headed in opposite directions down the corridor. Thaddeus strode up to the lounge door where he used his biometric ID to override the lockout, "bitches good!" he heard Ebenezer yell from his bedroom before entering the lounge and flicking the lights on "are you alive in there you fuck ugly slug!" he yelled as he approached the Perspex box, Fatty's face was barely distinguishable from the rest of his shredded body and the circular disks still whizzed efficiently, inches deep into his flesh "fuck me, it must have been fun getting thrown around in there" Thaddeus laughed admiring the fresh lacerations in fatty's body "you still with us or is it your lucky day?" he yelled into the box, a mouthful of blood and pus suddenly erupted from what must have been fatty's gob and he gasped frantically as he tried to take in air "ah ha ha" Thaddeus laughed as he pushed the intercom button "well even I think you've had enough of the circular saw blades for one sitting, let's try something else" he pressed the circular saw button and the blades retracted slowly from Fatty's torso, in his constant agonising pain the fat shit hardly noticed their absence "let's give this one a go" Thaddeus said inquisitively as he pressed one marked "hyperbaric", "it'll take couple of hours but pretty soon the inside of that box will be so pressurised you will swell up to the size of an air balloon and explode, that is of course if I dont turn it off just before you pop" he laughed and strode out of the room toward the elevator.

"Waqa, how long do you think this will take to repair?" Ebenezer asked as the crew surveyed the trashed cargo bay "I dunno man" Waqa replied as he looked around shaking his head "we've got a busted engine, numerous areas of the hull have been compromised and above all that you fellas will need a new car. I think about 2 weeks", "shit!" Ebenezer yelled as he kicked a dead gang member out of the loading ramp "well at least you two can finally take some time to recover" Mya said as she dabbed Thaddeus's bloody forehead with a towel "Core" Thaddeus said suddenly, can you take a look at something in the meantime?" he pointed to the laptop which was now upside down in the centre of the room "I'm pretty sure its smashed to fuck but if you can get anything out of it.." Core nodded and grabbed the laptop "I'll see what I can do" he replied as he hurried into the elevator. "Well," Thaddeus said as he stood up and walked toward Ebenezer "I guess it's time to break open the cognac" Mya rolled her eyes and tutted loudly.

CHAPTER 11: BAD TO THE BONE.

Location: London

Date: June 28th, 2035

Time: 0700hrs

"**F**uckinghell, bro are you alright? Ive been looking for you everywhere" Ebenezer's voice echoed in the darkness. Thaddeus slowly opened his eyes and like a police officer hiding behind the corner the worst hangover in the world leapt into his head "ughhhh" he groaned "where the fuck am I?" Ebenezer's laughter could be heard echoing off the walls around him. "Bro you're in the fucking rubbish chute, Ive been searching the entire ship trying to find you", Thaddeus focused on the aluminium walls around him and realised he was upside down "what the fuck?, pull me out!" he called behind him, Ebenezer reached down the chute and grabbed Thaddeus by the ankle "your fucking nuts bro" he chuckled as he slowly pulled him out "why the fuck did you choose to sleep down there of all places?", Thaddeus groaned loudly as Ebenezer helped him out of the rubbish chute "I dunno" he moaned as he put his hands to his throbbing head "but I wish you would have left me down there my fucking cranium is on fire", "well it's a good thing I didn't because I was about to hit the eject button and if you would draw your attention to the window you will see that we are currently airborne". Thaddeus staggered to the window and peered out into the clouds "fuck me how long have I been out?" he asked, "bro you've been pounding whiskey and cognac for ten days straight, a few nights ago you said you were going to go and decapitate Fatty and just disappeared", "Fuck!" Thaddeus yelled "I fucking forgot about that cunt!" he stormed down the corridor in the direction of the lounge "wait, wait" Ebenezer called behind him "your fucking lucky mate I turned down the pressure just in time, the fat shit was about to explode so relax" Thaddeus gasped in relief "hes still alive then?" he asked "yup I force fed him some more rat shit and turned the circulars back on, he should be good for another week or so", "thank fuck bro, thank you so much" Thaddeus said gratefully giving his brother a high five "and thats not all" Ebenezer continued "Ive got a surprise for you, follow me down to the garage, you'll fucking love this".

Waqa waqa had an enormous grin on his grid as he greeted the brothers at the bottom of the elevator "my homie, come right this way" he said as he put an arm around Thaddeus's shoulder "have I got a special treat in store for you, me and Ebenezer have been working on this the last few days" he led Thaddeus to the other end of the garage where a large white sheet was draped over an object. "what's this?" Thaddeus asked, his hangover being slowly replaced by intrigue, Ebenezer grinned "may I do the honours Waqa?" he asked "go right on ahead my friend" the giant replied "check this out bro" Ebenezer said with a grin before yanking the sheet off in one swift movement, Thaddeus's jaw dropped at what stood before him.

The Harley Davidson was immaculate, the paintjob was jet with gold flames and the chrome components shone fantastically in the light, the saddle was fashioned from buffalo hide and welded to the frame of the bike was a sidecar with a matching paint job. "fuck me!" Thaddeus gasped in amazement "this is fucking insane" he walked over to the bike and put his hand on the gorgeous saddle "fuckinghell it even has an air con!" "yup" Ebenezer beamed proudly "and you can even set it to Rich", "whoa!" Thaddeus exclaimed "is this a fucking MG42?" he asked as he examined the machine gun mounted to the front of the side car "yeah that was my idea" Ebenezer replied "I nicked it from the imperial war museum before we left "man I can't wait to mow some fuckers down with this bad boy" Thaddeus continued as he patted the barrel of the gun. "theres something else" Ebenezer exclaimed "Core, he found something on the laptop, hes downloaded it to our PDA's I thought I'd wait until I found you before I took a look" Thaddeus wiped dried vomit from the screen of the PDA on his forearm and clicked the upload button on the screen "oh fuck! this is a fucking jackpot bro!" he said excitedly "what, what is it?" Ebenezer said, looking at his own PDA a list of names began to scroll down his screen.

The Doctor

Head of R.I.S.E

Location: Unknown

The Dean himself

Head of Oxford university (impeccable sense of style).

Location: Oxford

Mark Langley

CEO of Kortex industries.

location: London

Frederick von Klausner

Operations manager, nuclear power.

location: Dampierre, France

Jimmy Whizz

Distributor of narcotic known as Zial.

Location: the local bin site, Abingdon.

"Fuck me, is this what I think it is?" Ebenezer asked, "it sure is" Thaddeus replied as he studied the names "this is a list of R.I.S.E inner circle members", "at least we can cross half these mother fuckers off the list" Ebenezer replied through a grin "hang on whos this asshole?" Thaddeus asked as he stopped on a name "Frederick Von Klausner, who the fuck is that?" "beats me" Ebenezer shrugged "but if I had to take a wild guess, I'd say it's probably the next guy well put in the ground" Thaddeus nodded in response "alright, is that useless robot back in the driving seat?" "afraid so" Ebenezer replied grimly. Thaddeus sighed loudly before pressing a button on the side of his headset "Goffbot, are you reading me?" Thaddeus spoke into his mike. "uhh yes boss, here boss" the idiotic voice crackled in response in Thaddeus's ear canal "listen carefully" Thaddeus instructed "set co-ordinates for Dampierre in France, anywhere where theres a high volume of nuclear activity", "uhh roger boss, setting co-ordinates to McDonalds now boss". Thaddeus bellowed in anger. "Fucking listen! I said Dampierre in fucking France now have you got that?", "uhh yes boss Dampierre, France boss" the Goffbot responded, Thaddeus shook his head in disbelief "that fucking useless piece of shit" he said angrily, his hangover starting to reappear. "Come on" Ebenezer called as he walked toward the lift "lets get to the armoury and load up, it's time we pay this Klausner fucker a visit, maybe he can lead us to the dean or even this doctor son of a bitch". Thaddeus followed behind him "when I get my hands on this doctor asshole, I'm going to skin him alive" he said through gritted teeth "your fucking telling me bro" Ebenezer replied "I'm gonna castrate the mother fucker".

CHAPTER 12: "PAS DE REDDITION".

Location: Dampierre, France

Date: June 29th, 2035

Time: 02:50 hrs

Thunder boomed and lightning streaked through the night sky as the Harley Davidson roared through the snowy mountains on the approach to the Dampierre Nuclear Power facility, "I can't believe that idiot robot crashed into the Eiffel Tower!" Thaddeus yelled over the engine, "how much further!?" he called from the sidecar. Ebenezer looked down at his PDA and shook the rain from the screen "thirty minutes!" he yelled back "but if you want a more spirited ride, I can get us there in fifteen", "fuck it" Thaddeus replied, "punch it!", Ebenezer twisted the throttle wide open, the bike snarled into life as the turbos began spooling up and whistling away, the brothers sped down the twisty roads at an immense pace. Slowly but surely the enormous silhouette of the facility loomed into view.

"you ready for this?" Ebenezer asked as the bike came to a stop at the facility's entrance "lets fucking do it" Thaddeus replied as he cocked the MG42. "The place looks fucking abandoned" Ebenezer remarked as he dismounted from the bike "alright I'm gonna try and get this open, cover me with the 42", Ebenezer cocked his tommy gun and advanced to a large steel blast door which covered the entrance of the building " ah fucking hell!" he yelled back to Thaddeus "its fucking welded shut bro I can't open it" "no problem" Thaddeus yelled back I'll do a quick scan and see what we're working with. Thaddeus engaged his shoulder mounted scanner and scanned the iron door. "right, it's like a bank vault door bro it's got locking bolts in 12 places, were going to have to blow it open", "I was hoping you'd say that" Ebenezer replied, a huge grin spreading across his face "here catch" Thaddeus yelled as he threw Ebenezer a satchel charge. Ebenezer rammed the charge in the doors mechanism and took cover behind a nearby concrete pillar. Thaddeus watched as he pulled a solid gold detonator from a pocket in his Kevlar armor, "ready for some fireworks!?" he yelled, before Thaddeus could answer Ebenezer hit the detonator and an enormous blast filled the air, the door flew from its recess and was flung skyward until it came crashing down landing in a heap of twisted metal on the snow-covered floor.

"Fuck me!" Thaddeus yelled as he waved the smoke from in front of him "you ok?"

Ebenezer emerged from behind the pillar coughing and laughing at the same time "fuckinghell, we keep those things in the airship?" he called to Thaddeus. Suddenly the tunnel which the door had guarded lit up and the shadows of approaching troops could be seen dancing across the walls "fuck!" Thaddeus yelled as he swiveled the machine gun to point down the tunnel. "bro we've got incoming, looks like this place isn't deserted after all!" just as he said that bullets ripped through the air toward him, Thaddeus yelled as he unleashed hell with the MG42 pumping round after round into the soldiers who emerged from the tunnels entrance. Ebenezer sprinted back to the bike and hit the prone position next to Thaddeus returning fire wildly with his tommy gun. "Fuck me" he yelled over the gunfire "there's fucking loads of them!" just then a bullet ripped into his shoulder and Ebenezer yelled in pain, "mother fucker!" he screamed as he rolled on the floor in agony, his blood staining the snow around him.

Thaddeus was in fierce battle with the troops that slowly advanced on the brother's position, finally the shooting stopped. "There out of ammo lets fucking go!" he unsheathed his golden machete from his back and ran toward the remaining guards Ebenezer jumped up and followed Thaddeus, the guards dropped their empty weapons and ran screaming into the tunnel, the espartano brothers ran after them and confronted the men who started to plead for their lives pathetically.

Thaddeus leapt forward and drove his machetes blade though a guard's throat "stop fucking winging!" he shouted into the guards face as he twisted the blade "your all gonna fucking die so shut up and have some dignity", Ebenezer quickly dispatched the remaining guards as he swung his machete through the air violently.

"let's move" Thaddeus said as he cleaned the blood from his machetes blade "the whole place will be crawling with guards any second, let's keep moving and find this Klausner piece of shit". Ebenezer reloaded his tommy gun and tossed Thaddeus a FAMAS assault rifle he pulled from a wall mounted rack. "I think its this way" he replied as he opened a door to the side of tunnel.

"Refinery" a sign read printed on the door in yellow letters.

The two brothers entered a large room filled with huge vats of purple liquid which bubbled away, the occasional splash from one of the vats would hit the floor and burn a hole straight through the concrete. The smell was awful and the brothers both gagged as they donned their respirators. Thaddeus went in closer to find out what the liquid was "that's strange" he said as he conducted a scan, "I've got no files on this substance?", "impossible!" Ebenezer said as he joined him "what does that mean?", "it means that it's not anything known in the whole galaxy" Thaddeus replied, "this is a big problem who knows how long they have been making this and god knows what it's used for".

Suddenly a door slammed open and armed men ran in firing, Thaddeus and Ebenezer ran at the guards like men possessed firing their machine guns and bellowing as they advanced, Thaddeus took a gunshot to the leg and screamed in pain as he fell to the floor. Ebenezer grabbed one of the guards and started pounding his face into the ground, rounds bounced off his amour plated back as he did so "son of a bitch!" Thaddeus yelled as he got to his feet and continued firing "theses fuckers are never ending there must be hundreds of them!" the brothers fought on, Ebenezer was amidst the chaos, punching and slicing with his meat cleaver like a madman, one by one the guards were executed until finally not one of them was left standing.

Blood and shredded flesh stained the concrete floor. Ebenezer admired the dead bodies scattered all over the room "bro it looks like a baby threw all its toys out the pram but instead of toys its dead people" he laughed, "fancy throwing some bodies into the purple liquid to see what happens?", "fucking right I do!" Thaddeus shouted excitedly in response. Ebenezer grabbed one of the dead bodies and walked towards an open vat, "here goes nothing" he said excitedly as he threw the lifeless body into the liquid. With a loud hiss the body instantly vaporized on contact "wow! again again!" shouted Thaddeus grinning ear to ear Ebenezer picked up another body by its face "bro you have a go!" he said dumping the body in Thaddeus's arms. Thaddeus grabbed the body and slowly dipped its head into the bubbling purple liquid, to his total enjoyment the man's skull instantly disintegrated "come on we'll be here all day we have a mission to do" Thaddeus said as he cocked his rifle. Looking like an upset child Ebenezer let out a loud sigh and checked his tommy guns magazine, "I'm sure there will be more people to throw in bro, but let's find this son of a bitch first". Thaddeus said empathetically.

The brothers quickly moved from the room into a steel-clad corridor "we must be getting closer" Thaddeus said as he looked around "there's cameras everywhere down here" Ebenezer ran up to one of the cameras and ripped it off the wall, "were coming for you Klausner your fucking dead meat!" he yelled into the camera, he bit the lens clean off and spat it out on the floor. The two brothers continued down the corridor until they reached a large open room with what looked like metal storage boxes stacked up on one side "hold up…you hear that?" Thaddeus said stopping suddenly at the rooms entrance. "what is it" Ebenezer asked quietly taking aim with his tommy gun, "stay frosty" Thaddeus replied, we could be walking into an ambush. Slowly the brothers advanced into the room and crept through the storage units. All of a sudden, a voice yelled through the air, "open fire!!", an enormous hail of bullets erupted from the side of the room. "fuck!!" Ebenezer yelled as the Espartano brothers adopted the kneeling position and returned fire into the direction of the storage boxes "were sitting ducks, we need to get the fuck into cover!" Thaddeus yelled over the roar of the gunfire, soldiers emerged from behind the storage boxes and advanced toward the brothers, bullets ripped through Ebenezer's Kevlar and penetrated his flesh, he roared loudly still continuing to engage the enemy, "I'm out!" Thaddeus yelled, he threw the FAMAS aside and drew his magnificent machete before running into the hellfire of battle screaming as he charged, the soldiers opened fire as he advanced, rounds whizzed through the air hitting Thaddeus in multiple locations before he reached them. Thaddeus spat blood into the first man's face before decapitating him in an instant. Ebenezer slung his tommy gun and drew his own machete joining Thaddeus in the bloodbath, swooshing and swiping the brothers slashed the soldiers open sending guts and limbs everywhere, slowly the body's piled up until only one was left alive, "please" the soldier begged as he crawled across the floor leaving a trail of his own blood. Thaddeus strode over to him holding his own guts in place with his hand "where the fuck is he?" he yelled as he kicked the helpless man onto his back, the guard let out a bloodcurdling scream as Thaddeus jammed his machete into the man's groin "I can't fucking hear you, where is Klausner?" the soldier pointed to a large blast door at the end of the room which suddenly began to open "fuck!" Thaddeus yelled as he stamped the man's brains into the metal floor "bro grab a weapon quick, there's fucking more of them coming!" Ebenezer staggered to Thaddeus picking up an assault rifle on the way, another squad of soldiers began to fill the room, "there's too fucking many of them" he replied slumping to his knees as blood spurted from the various bullet holes in his body "we can fucking take them!" Thaddeus yelled through gritted teeth "c'mon let's do this" he reached down and helped Ebenezer to his feet and the brothers took cover behind one of the storage boxes. "Ok" Ebenezer groaned as he cocked his rifle "lets waste these pussies" Thaddeus and Ebenezer exchanged a bloody high five and watched from cover as what must have been two hundred heavily armed soldiers got into formation before them.

"hold fire" a voice suddenly called out from behind the squad, slowly an officer stepped out in front of the soldiers and began to speak "I'm Major Pierre Brannigan, your outnumbered and outgunned, don't be foolish, drop your weapons and surrender now or my men will fill you with lead", "no fucking surrender"

Thaddeus whispered to Ebenezer, Ebenezer nodded in response, "I'm going to give you to the count of ten, then we will open fire" The officer continued, "how about we see you in fucking hell!" Thaddeus yelled back as the two brothers broke cover and charged toward the sea of troopers firing wildly as they ran. Bullets ripped into the Major Brannigan and he fell to his knees with a gurgle, the soldiers returned fire and bullets whizzed over the brother's heads as they continued their advance "you mother fuckers!" Ebenezer screamed as he pumped round after round into the squad before him "Ebenezer!" Thaddeus yelled, Ebenezer looked at Thaddeus and watched in horror as a bullet ripped through his brothers neck spraying blood everywhere. "Nooo!" Ebenezer bellowed as he caught Thaddeus before he hit the floor, he looked at Thaddeus and saw him grin one last time before whispering "what a hoot" before closing his eyes forever.

CHAPTER 13: DIRT NAP.

Location: Dampierre, France

Date: June 29th, 2035

Time: 03:30 hrs

Ebenezer was hit twice in the back as he dragged his dead brother back into cover behind the storage box. "fuck fuck no!!" he shouted as the bullets continued to slice through the air above him, Ebenezer slapped Thaddeus "brother fucking stay with me, fucking wake up!" he looked down and saw the huge hole in his brothers' neck, blood gushing out at a rapid rate. Ebenezer reached for his trauma kit and pulled out bandages and pads he tried in vain to stop the bleeding whilst raising his rifle to give returning fire as the soldiers who advanced on his position "fuck you, you mother fuckers!" he yelled.

"Ebenezer" a robotic voice suddenly crackled through his headset, "you don't have much time, the small access panel behind you, rip it off and drop down the vent", Ebenezer put a hand to his headset "who the fuck is this?" he yelled over the gunfire, "no time to explain, do what I say or your dead, I can help you and your brother, now hurry" the voice continued. Ebenezer let rip the last of his magazine over the storage crate into the incoming soldiers before turning and ripping the access panel off the wall "don't worry bro, hang in there I'm getting you out of here" he said frantically as he pushed Thaddeus through the hole where he dropped into the vent below.

"Son of a bitch!" Ebenezer yelled as he landed on top of Thaddeus a couple of levels down, "good" the voice crackled back into Ebenezer's ear "at the end of the corridor is a blast door, move quickly I can only open it for a second then it will close, hurry the soldiers are back on your position" Ebenezer tossed his rifle and slung Thaddeus onto his shoulders "Cmon!" he screamed as he ran painfully down the corridor toward the blast door which began to open. The soldiers dropped from the vent and began firing as Ebenezer ran as fast as his injuries would permit him "arrrgh!" he screamed as another bullet struck him in the thigh, he just made it through the blast door as he was hit once more in the back causing him to drop Thaddeus into the blast room and slump onto his knees, "closing blast doors now" the voice continued, the door behind him slowly shut as rounds bounced off it "don't worry, that's a level 9 security door, they wont be able to get in, and you wont be able to get out" the voice said with a sinister streak in its mechanical voice. "who the fuck are you?" Ebenezer groaned as he slumped against the wall of the blast room. "lights on!" the voice said suddenly. Ebenezer shielded his eyes as the room lit up with bright white

fluorescent lighting, Ebenezer put his hand over his eyes as he adjusted to the brightness. "help Thaddeus" he coughed, blood pouring from his nostrils "in time" the voice cooed smoothly "but first, cast your attention to the other side of the room" Ebenezer squinted through the light and could see a figure sitting in an office chair with his back to him. "Well, you wanted him, here he is, may I present to you Frederick Von Klausner" the voice echoed, this time from speakers in the room.

Ebenezer slowly stood to his knees and unsheathed his machete "mother fucker" he muttered as he slowly approached the chair "my fucking brother died for you? tell me where the doctor is you cunt!" Ebenezer span the chair around and was shocked at what he saw. Klausner's throat was cut from ear to ear, his ghost white face contorted in a horrific expression. "what the fuck?" Ebenezer said in a confused whisper.

Suddenly a metal shutter on the opposite wall whizzed open to reveal a viewing window into a dark room, a silhouette of a figure could be seen behind the glass "what the fucks going on?" Ebenezer demanded "who the fuck are you?". "Tut tut tut poor Thaddeus all torn up" a human voice echoed from the speakers; Ebenezer was consumed by rage "you cunt how dare you who the fuck are you? tell me before I fucking end you!" Ebenezer punched the glass with his robotic hand, but it was useless "so very predictable" the voice continued "all braun and no brains" Ebenezer gazed into the window, as the lights inside flickered on, he instantly recognized the figure before him.

Fresh Italian suit, handmade leather shoes and a wafer-thin solid gold watch with matching cuff links. "You!" Ebenezer yelled as the Dean of Oxford university smiled back at him "we have a winner" the smooth voice of the dean cooed through the speakers. "you son of a bitch ill fucking…!", "sit down Ebenezer" the dean interrupted "Ill explain this in a way even you can understand, oh and don't worry about Thaddeus, vitals show he's already dead" Ebenezer put his head in his hands and slumped back against the wall, "you see" the dean continued as he ran his fingers through his chestnut brown hair "Klausner was an egotistical greedy son of a bitch and I couldn't risk someone like that moving in on my position as number two in R.I.S.E, so here's what happened, you and your brother stormed this facility, killing everybody and executing Klausner,

unfortunately, neither you or anybody else escaped the facility before it went into meltdown where everybody was killed, oh and of course I was never here" The dean looked at his watch "and on that note, I better get a move on, I have a helicopter to catch, good luck", the dean turned and headed to an elevator door behind him "wait" Ebenezer said suddenly "oh I'm sorry" the dean replied "final words, how rude of me, go ahead", "see you in fucking hell" Ebenezer said coldly, the dean smirked and adjusted his tie "well you'll have to wait for me I'm afraid" he checked his watch once more "you'll be there soon" he turned and entered the elevator waving sarcastically as he ascended to the roof. "fuck!" Ebenezer yelled as he struggled to his feet "CORE MELTDOWN IN T-MINUS 3 MINUTES" a computerized warning bellowed from the rooms speakers, Ebenezer staggered to The blast door and tried in vain to pull it open "mother fucker!" he yelled against the strain before collapsing on the floor next to Thaddeus's motionless body "bro" he said through tears as he unsheathed his machete "I'm fucking sorry" he laid the golden weapon on his brothers chest and lay next to him, blood poured from his wounds as he stared up at the flashing red warning lights on the ceiling "CORE MELTDOWN IN T-MINUS 1 MINUTE" the computerized voice echoed through the room which began to spin as Ebenezer's life slipped away. "this is it" he thought "what a fucking knees up", "CORE MELTDOWN IMMINENT" The room shook, and Ebenezer shut his eyes for the last time.

CHAPTER 14: TIME TO KILL.

Location: Unknown

Date: Unknown

Time: Unknown

The early morning sunlight shone through the trees and reflected brightly on the forest floor, sunbeams danced majestically on the mossy ground, slowly drying the dewdrops left by the early morning mist, and with it came an earthy yet natural aroma to the morning air. the calming silence was only broken by the occasional chatter of birds and slowly the creatures of the woods began to awaken and start their rituals for their day.

Ebenezer awoke with a jump and reached instantly for his sidearm which was not there, he slowly sat up and realised he was dressed in a totally silver body suit with only his head, hands and feet uncovered, "what the hell?" he muttered as he stood up and surveyed his surroundings, he appeared to be in a vast forest with trees that seemed to go on for miles, Autumn leaves crunched under his bare feet and he slowly stepped forward "where the fuck am I?" he muttered as he tried to regain his balance "Thaddeus!" he yelled, his voice echoed into the forest for what sounded like an infinite distance, he wiped his face and realised his cybernetic hand had vanished and had instead been replaced by a human one once more "holy shit, what the fucks going on?" he said out loud as he gently touched his new appendage. "I think were dreaming" a dazed voice called from the trees behind him, Ebenezer spun around and saw in relief that not too far away Thaddeus was slowly standing to his feet, he noticed he was dressed exactly the same as him and that his cybernetic implants were also missing "what the fuck" Thaddeus said loudly in a shocked voice "where the fuck are we and look at us? your hands back to normal and look at my fucking face!" Ebenezer continued to examine his now human hand, "fuck me!" he yelled back with a grin "I can jerk off again! ", Thaddeus walked toward him, the leaves crunching under his feet "we better get out of here bro, we need to get back to the airship" Ebenezer nodded in response "let's move" he said in agreement.

The two men walked through the woods all the while complaining about the lack of Drexel's or footwear in the situation, only stopping to moan or practise hand to hand combat they walked for miles. "Fuckinghell when does this place end!" Ebenezer said in a frustrated tone, "do you remember anything?" he asked suddenly stopping "all I remember is blackness" Thaddeus replied, "did we get on the whiskey again?" Ebenezer asked, Thaddeus shook his head "No way, theres no whores lying around and my Gulliver feels absolutely fine, in fact I feel better than I think ive ever felt," Ebenezer nodded "me too mate, what the fuck happened" they continued walking for another few hours trying to piece together the events that brought them here but to no avail. Suddenly Thaddeus stopped in his tracks, "Bro look!" he said pointing into the forest "what? I can't see shit" Ebenezer replied as he attempted to follow Thaddeus's finger "there!" Thaddeus said excitedly "theres a building! ", in the distance Ebenezer could just make out what looked like a log cabin in a clearing, "thank fuck!" Ebenezer said triumphantly, "let's go, hopefully theres some Drexel's in there" he said as he started walking hurriedly toward the cabin, Thaddeus chuckled and followed behind.

It was a simple structure with one window and a door that was bolted shut, ancient logs surrounded the small cabin and overgrown ivy had emerged from cracks in the floorboards of the dilapidated porch, a broken chair swing swung loosely from a shackle attached to the porches ceiling and rays of sunlight shone through the gaps in the woodwork.

"Hello!" Ebenezer bellowed as he reached the edge of the clearing "anyone home?" he called again, "no answer" he called back to Thaddeus with a shrug "fuck it lets get in there before nightfall" Thaddeus said impatiently as he waded his way through dead leaves and arrived at the clearing. "Who do you think lives here?" Ebenezer asked as they approached the cabins door "beats me" Thaddeus replied as he grabbed the bolt "but it better not be some inbred mother fucker looking for a good time" Ebenezer laughed as Thaddeus yanked the door open and stepped inside "fuckinghell!" Thaddeus yelled in total surprise, Ebenezer stepped inside the cabin and joined his brother in complete shock.

The interior of the cabin was absolutely stocked full of supplies, crates of the finest whiskey known to man were stacked to ceiling height either side of a back door which stood on the opposite side of the room. There was a beautifully crafted oak table and chair set in the centre of the cabin which was piled high with fresh cartons of cigarettes and a vintage red radio, from the ceiling hung a diamond chandelier and on the rooms opposite wall stood a magnificent fireplace. The two men stood in shock for at least a minute before Ebenezer finally spoke "what the fuck?" he gasped, he slowly took a seat at the table and reached for a pack of cigarettes "Thaddeus walked to the corner of the room and picked a bottle of whiskey from one of the crates "bro, who the fuck lives here? he asked unscrewing the lid of the bottle, Ebenezer turned and grinned whilst lighting a cigarette with a solid gold zippo he had found on the table. "we do" he replied, Thaddeus exhaled blissfully and took a generous swig of the whiskey "hey Ebenezer turn that radio on, maybe well get an idea of where the fuck we are", "good idea!" Ebenezer replied as he grabbed the radio and clicked a white knob clockwise, a loud crackle emitted from the radios speaker and Ebenezer tried in vain to tune it to a channel, "fucking thing" he said angrily, suddenly through the crackles a distorted voice could be heard "BZZZ BEGINNING THE BZZZZZ CEREBRAL UPLOAD" it crackled "IMPORTANT BZZZZZ YOU MUST ACTIVATE BZZZZZZ FROM INSIDE BZZZZZ CODING BACKDOOR BZZZZZZ BZZZZZ UNLOCK 1 WEEK BZZZZZ, Ebenezer looked at Thaddeus "did you get any of that?" he asked "not a word" Thaddeus replied taking another gulp of whiskey, Ebenezer threw the radio over his shoulder where it smashed to pieces against the back door of the cabin. Thaddeus brought the bottle of whiskey to the table and helped himself to a Drexel, "I dont get it" he said as he slumped into the armchair opposite his brother "All that walking and I'm still not hungry at all", "me neither" Ebenezer replied "probably a good thing, theres not a crumb of food in the entire cabin" Thaddeus said as he looked around the room "I'll get that fire going, it's got be close to nightfall" Ebenezer grunted as he stood up from the armchair, "weird" Thaddeus exclaimed as looked towards the window", "it's still so bright outside". Finally, Ebenezer got the fire lit and now he had slumped back into the armchair and was opening a fresh pack of cigarettes "fancy a swig?" Thaddeus asked gesturing the bottle in Ebenezer's direction "when in Rome" Ebenezer replied with a grin, "just a few though, we could be here for some time and we dont the supplies to run dry too soon", "of course" Thaddeus replied handing him a bottle of whiskey. "this is fucking good shit" Ebenezer exclaimed whilst admiring the bottle "I know" Thaddeus replied "it's my favourite whiskey too,

Lords ambrosia" Ebenezer suddenly looked confused "this is fucking weird" he said "these are my favourite variety of Drexel's, do you reckon whoever owns this place is related to us?" Thaddeus thought about it for a second and after a drag he responded, "fuck knows who it is but with taste like this we should offer him a job on the airship" Ebenezer nodded in agreement "Oh fuck!" Thaddeus suddenly yelled grabbing the bottle and jumping to his feet "bro the fucking airship!" Ebenezer leapt up in shock. "Where the fuck did we leave it?" Thaddeus asked frantically "fuck!" Ebenezer said loudly "I remember something, like a fucking explosion" Thaddeus started pacing up and down the cabin slapping his forehead in an attempt to remember "think, think" he said to himself, he took a large gulp of the whiskey and threw the empty bottle across the room "your right!" he said after a few moments "I remember falling", fuckinghell you dont think...." "The airship!" Ebenezer interrupted his face white with shock. Thaddeus grabbed another bottle of scotch and turned to face his brother "bro" he said quietly "I think were fucking dead".

CHAPTER 15: QUANTUM SLEEP.

Location: Unknown

Date: Unknown

Time: Unknown

The early morning sunlight shone through the trees and reflected brightly on the forest floor, sunbeams danced majestically on the mossy ground and Ebenezer laughed hysterically as he danced like a madman in the never ending daylight of the clearing, inside the cabin Thaddeus who had equally lost his mind frantically scribbled into his diary "today marks 8 years!, 8 fucking years we've been here and it still makes no sense!!, never hungry, never tired, for fucks sake it's never fucking night time!!" he screamed as he threw his diary across the room and flung the table across the room where it smashed into the enormous pile of empty bottles and cigarette packets that had nearly completely hidden the back door from view, he grabbed an empty bottle of whiskey from the pile and stared longingly into the bottle, the whiskey and cigarettes had run out years ago but it didn't matter as the two brothers never became thirsty. Thaddeus smashed the bottle into his face to no effect "I can't even die!!" he screamed whilst wrenching the cabin door open "Ebenezer!" he bellowed "I'm going, I can't fucking take it" Ebenezer laughed even louder "pointless!" he yelled as he skipped around the perimeter of the clearing "I know, I fucking know!" Thaddeus yelled back as he hung his head in despair and began weeping, Ebenezer was right, no matter what direction you walked, as soon as you hit the 7-mile mark you'd be right back at the clearing again face to face with the log cabin of doom "fuck it!!" Thaddeus screamed as he turned and re-entered the cabin slamming the living shit out of the door as he did so, he slumped into the oak armchair for the millionth time and put his head in his hands, "pointless!" Ebenezer laughed as he skipped past the window ", "this is hell" Thaddeus said defeatedly "we fucking died, and this is hell".

With a bang that made Thaddeus nearly jump out of his skin Ebenezer kicked the door clean off its hinges and stomped into the log cabin "dance with me!" he yelled to Thaddeus, Thaddeus leapt to his feet and marched over to him "I'm not in the fucking mood to dance!" he yelled "why dont you sit down and stop fucking around!" Ebenezer looked hurt and after a moments pause, he pushed past him toward the armchair "fuck" Thaddeus said quietly, his voice full of regret as Ebenezer slumped into the seat. Thaddeus walked to Ebenezer and put his hand on his shoulder "bro, look I'm fucking sorry, this place..." Ebenezer slapped his hand away and stood up "you think I'm not fucking sick of this place too!!" he yelled "I fucking hate this!, never fucking night time, never fucking sleep!, I haven't taken a shit in eight fucking years!", "bro calm down" Thaddeus started "no, Ive fucking had enough, this is bullshit!" he screamed as he flipped his armchair upside down and began wreaking havoc "fuck! bro chill the fuck out!" Thaddeus yelled stumbling backwards into the pile of rubbish behind him "dont tell me to fucking chill out!" Ebenezer roared as he lunged at Thaddeus, Thaddeus quickly rolled out of the way as Ebenezer leapt toward him smashing his fist past his head and through the back door "Listen!" Thaddeus shouted as Ebenezer slowly got to his feet "this isn't going to..." Thaddeus suddenly stopped short of what he was saying, and his jaw nearly hit the floor as he stared at Ebenezer "what the fuck, bro what the fuck? look at your hand!", "what?!" Ebenezer yelled impatiently looking down "wha..what the?! he joined Thaddeus in confused horror as he looked at his left arm and realised his hand and most of his forearm had completely vanished "what the fuck, what the fuck!" he repeated over and over again in panic. Thaddeus barged past him to the pile of rubbish and began chucking empty bottles across the room "help me!" he said hurriedly, Ebenezer used his remaining hand to pick up bottles and cigarette cartons and throw them aside "fuck me!" Thaddeus exclaimed in shock as he uncovered the back door "look!" he pointed at the hole Ebenezer had created in the door and looked into it "what the fucks going on!" Ebenezer wailed "bro I know what's happening! he yelled turning from the hole and excitedly grabbing Ebenezer by the shoulders, I know what's going on!!" Thaddeus got up and ran out of the front door and around the building "I'll be fucking dammed!" Ebenezer heard him say from the other side of the back door, "what is it?" Ebenezer called back "the hole is on this side too, bro stick your other arm through I want to test something" Thaddeus called, "fuck that!" Ebenezer yelled back "you fucking do it!" "fine!" Thaddeus yelled back. Ebenezer waited for the arm to come through, but it never appeared "bro?!" Ebenezer called after a few moments "what happened?" a few minutes passed as Ebenezer waited in anticipation when suddenly a creak on the porch caused him to spin around where to his horror, he saw the headless figure of Thaddeus slowly bump his way into the log cabin, "aaarggghhhh!!!" Ebenezer yelled jumping to his feet "bro what the fuck!" he yelled as he ran to Thaddeus's aid "shit! shit! shit!" he said as he led his headless brother to the un-flipped armchair, Thaddeus started waving his arms as he sat down and held up a hand to show the "OK" gesture "I dont understand?" Ebenezer gasped "what the fuck? what's going on?" Thaddeus pointed in a rough direction of the back door, Ebenezer looked at the door and back to Thaddeus who was now standing to his feet, his arm still outstretched "I dont get it, what do you want me to do?" Ebenezer called in desperation, Thaddeus charaded an opening action with his hand before pointing at the door once again "fucking gotcha!" Ebenezer said as he marched toward the door, he grabbed the ancient door handle with his remaining hand and pulled with all of his strength, inch by inch the door slowly creaked open and Ebenezer gasped as he saw what was behind it.

"fuckinghell!" he said slowly as he stepped back and gazed into the doorway, instead of there being the forest that stood behind the cabin it appeared that behind the door was nothing but pure whiteness that stretched on for an infinity, he turned and grabbed Thaddeus by the shoulders "bro what the fuck is that?!" he yelled forgetting Thaddeus could not hear him, Thaddeus pointed again at the door way and gestured Ebenezer to go through it, Ebenezer turned and gazed in horror at the endless void "fuck that!" he yelled, Thaddeus started walking toward the door and Ebenezer grabbed his arm to stop him "bro, what the fuck are you doing? theres nothing there, it's just an eternity of white!" Thaddeus kept advancing toward the door and Ebenezer dug his heels in "it's even worse than the cabin! bro stop!" he yelled in protest. Thaddeus stopped and turned his body to face Ebenezer's, awkwardly he put a hand on Ebenezer's shoulder and gave him the thumbs up with his other hand, even without his head Ebenezer knew what his brother was trying to say, "trust me bro". Thaddeus turned and walked slowly through the doorway where he vanished completely, Ebenezer paced up and down the room in a panic, his hand to his face. Suddenly he stopped and turned to face eternity. "Fuck it" he said after taking a deep breath, he ran and jumped through the doorway into nothingness.

CHAPTER 16: REGENERATION.

Location: The "Hungry Bird" airship

Date: December 3rd, 2043

Time: 18:15 hrs

COMMAND.COM

LOAD BIOS

MEMORY SET

SYSTEM STATUS

OK_

Ebenezer slowly opened his eyes and as he focused he recognised the familiar setting of the airships med bay in front of him "what the fuck?" he muttered groggily noticing his voice sounding different than usual, he tried to walk forward but was unable to as he was strapped vertically onto a surgical repair bed by titanium restraints, he looked down and realised he had been clothed in some sort of robotic armour "what the fucks going on?" he said again. "relax" a robotic voice similar to his own boomed from across the room, he looked around the room and saw only a large military grade assault droid strapped into a bed the same as his "who the fuck said that?!" Ebenezer bellowed as his eyes darted around the room trying to locate the source of the voice, the assault robot suddenly appeared to let out a sort of mechanical laugh "where the fuck is my brother? where's the rest of the fucking crew!?" Ebenezer yelled as he frantically fought against his restraints "let me the fuck out of here!" he yelled frantically "calm the fuck down bro" a loud voice could suddenly be heard from the direction of the assault robot. Ebenezer stopped and stared at the robot "T...Thaddeus?" he stuttered, the assault robot nodded its armoured video camera head in response, Ebenezer looked him up and down and took in the armoured torso sprayed with a black and white urban camouflage pattern, "bro what the fuck happened to you? and why the fuck am I in this suit?" he said looking down in confusion as he continued to struggle against his restraints. "Listen bro" Thaddeus whirred "you need to stay calm when I tell you this" Ebenezer looked back at him fearfully "what? what is it?" he asked anxiously "bro it's not a suit" Thaddeus replied, "it's you".

The Goffbot 4000 whirred into the room "the lords have awoken!" it chanted excitedly over and over as it span around 360 degrees. "please tell me what the fucks going on?" Ebenezer asked desperately as he looked down at his robotic torso, "try to think back" Mya responded as she entered the med bay behind the Goffbot "what do you remember?" she placed her steel clipboard down on a surgical table and walked over to Ebenezer "I... I remember an explosion" Ebenezer replied as he tried to think "and then waking up in the forest". "good" Mya responded as she checked his vitals "do you remember anything before that? do you remember finding Klaus or entering the powerplant? ", "fuck" Ebenezer said slowly as it started to come back to him, "what happened?" Mya took a deep breath and adjusted her glasses "it was a trap" she said before taking a deep breath "the bomb detonated and the nuclear reactor went critical, you and Thaddeus were killed instantly in the explosion", there was a long pause before Ebenezer spoke again "I..I dont get it, were here, I'm here, we spent years in that fucking cabin, please someone start talking sense " Mya put a hand on his robotic shoulder "it was core" she said "he downloaded your consciousness's into a virtual environment whilst he and myself worked on getting your new body's ready...only you never came back when you were supposed to, Core did try and reach you through the radio to instruct you that all you had to do was walk through the back door and you would come out of the simulation and be automatically uploaded into your new body's, why the fuck did it take you 8 years to do that? you were only supposed to be in there a week!" she said with a frustrated tone "do you have any idea what's happened since you've both been gone?, R.I.S.E has practically seized control of the world, theres nothing left!", "get us out of these restraints quick!" Thaddeus suddenly interrupted from across the room "theres something I need to do! ", "alright" Mya replied as she turned and began walking towards him "but take it steady" she warned "this might take you both some getting used to". She unclipped Thaddeus's restraints and he slowly exited the bed, his metal feet hit the floor with a loud "clank" and with the whirring of cybernetic components he awkwardly made his way out of the med bay and headed down the corridor in the direction of the lounge occasionally crashing into a wall as he walked causing the entire airship to rock, "let me go" Ebenezer said in a flat tone. Mya walked over and pressed a button on the side of the bed, the restraints instantly retracted. Ebenezer stepped out of the bed and nearly lost his balance as his feet hit the med bay floor "easy!" Mya said sternly "dont think about it, just try to act naturally" Ebenezer let out a mechanical grunt and steadied himself as he slowly walked toward the med bay mirror, once there he gazed in complete shock at his new body which, (apart from some minor details) was identical to Thaddeus.

he extended his pneumatic arms and made fists with his titanium fingers "this is insane" he said in an amazed cybernetic voice whilst admiring the blue and white urban camo patterned armour that covered his endoskeleton. Mya joined him at the mirror. "Before the shit really hit the fan with R.I.S.E, we received another coded message from MR. Red, he gave us the location of these two decommissioned assault droids which he hoped would help us in the attempt to regain control, of course once we realised, we could use them to host your consciousness we began the upload procedure immediately, look on the bright side" she continued whilst knocking on Ebenezer's armoured shoulder "at least your bulletproof".

CHAPTER 17: THE ALPHA AND THE OMEGA.

Location: The "Hungry Bird" airship

Date: December 3rd, 2043

Time: 20:00 hrs

Ebenezer awkwardly thumped into the lounge still trying to find his balance in his new body "bro what's up?" he asked Thaddeus was crouched in front of Fatty McKellar's perspex prison, "look" he replied, a hint of misery could be detected even in his robotic voice, Ebenezer stomped over and gazed into the box. The empty eye sockets of Fatty McKellar's shredded skeleton stared back at them, its toothless mouth was wide open, "ah fuck" Ebenezer said quietly "yup" Thaddeus replied, "eight years without feeding will do that", "actually" a voice suddenly called from behind them. Thaddeus and Ebenezer spun around to see Core standing in the doorway of the lounge "hes not technically dead" he continued as he walked toward the brothers "fuck me... Core, you haven't aged at all" Ebenezer gasped "it's my species", Core replied smugly,

" however no offense but you two look slightly different" he stood next to the brothers and peered into the glass, Thaddeus and Ebenezer looked at each other and although they could not express any facial expressions they were clearly confused. "not dead did you say?" Thaddeus asked, "No" Core continued "hes not totally dead anyway, I downloaded his consciousness much like I did with you two, I designed a program for him that im sure you would approve of, he is currently spending eternity in his own log cabin however I changed a couple of things, for example theres no back door... or front door for that matter, oh and the cabin is permanently ablaze, its crazy really, 5 years in and he still hasn't stopped screaming, he burns all day and night and just when hes about to turn to ash his body is reconstructed and he suffers all over again, I'll send a copy of the program to your PDA's so you can watch if you ever get bored. Thaddeus beamed with joy "fucking legend!" he roared with laughter and slapped Ebenezer a high five. "Now" Core continued "why on earth did it take you so long to figure out the back door?", "uhh yeah, let's not go there" Ebenezer replied, Thaddeus shook his head in response. "fair enough, well I think its time I showed you the machine" Core said as he headed toward the door "coming?", Thaddeus got to his feet "machine? What machine?", Core laughed "well you didn't think I would just let the Dean get away with it did you, come on" Thaddeus and Ebenezer looked at each other and followed him out of the room.

"Come in" Core said as he opened the door to his room. The two brothers lumbered inside and were astounded at what stood before them. In the centre of the room was a huge circular metal structure, wires poured from every recess and a low hum could be heard echoing around the room. "What the fuck is that?" Ebenezer asked as he approached the structure "don't touch!" Core warned, "this is my latest invention, it's a time dispersal chamber, the only one in existence, when you both uhh died, we contacted Mr. Red who sent us the relevant schematics and parts to construct this gateway "fuck me!" Ebenezer said in an amazed voice "um, what does it do?", Core took a deep breath "in the simplest terms this is a time machine", "whoa!" Thaddeus yelled "don't get too excited" Core replied, its taken years to gather enough plutonium and analyse the fibres of the space time continuum in order to make it ready, and it is ready, but for one trip there and one trip back only", "fuck me we could go back and kill Hitler bro!" Thaddeus exclaimed excitedly. "listen" Ebenezer began as he put a robotic hand on Thaddeus's shoulder "there will be plenty of time in the future for that but right now the worlds got a new asshole to deal with, we need to find this doctor son of a bitch and rip his head off", "ok" Thaddeus replied in a slightly disappointed tone "where did you have in mind?" Ebenezer grinned to himself "Core, power this thing up, I know exactly where to go". Core smiled and hit a green button, he stood back and watched as the time displacement chamber slowly flashed an electric shade of blue. "Oh I nearly forgot" he said suddenly "open that locker behind you Thaddeus" he instructed "Ive put together a little welcome home gift for you both.

CHAPTER 18: STITCH IN TIME.

Location: Dampierre, France

June 29th, 2035

Time 03:25 hrs

Ebenezer groaned as he cocked his rifle "lets waste these pussies". Thaddeus and Ebenezer exchanged a high five and watched from cover as what must have been two hundred heavily armed soldiers got into formation before them.

"hold fire" a voice suddenly called out from behind the squad, slowly an officer stepped out in front of the soldiers and began to speak "I'm Major Pierre Brannigan, your outnumbered and outgunned, don't be foolish, drop your weapons and surrender now or my men will fill you with lead", "no fucking surrender" Thaddeus whispered to Ebenezer, Ebenezer nodded in response. "I'm going to give you to the count of ten, then we will open fire" The officer continued.

Suddenly from the opposite side of the room a deafening blast of static electricity could be heard, the espartano brothers and the soldiers in front of them quickly shielded their eyes as a huge electric blue circle of what looked like plasma began to form in the middle of the room. "What the fuck!?" Ebenezer yelled over the noise trying to squint at the unfolding vortex in front of them "what the fuck is that!?" "look!" Thaddeus yelled back, the electric blue lightening had changed from the shape of a circle into a sphere which was whizzing around at a fantastic speed, huge arcs of electricity shot around the room "get down!" Major Brannigan screamed as twisted lightening shot into his squad instantly vaporizing a handful of soldiers. "what the fuck is going on?" Thaddeus yelled over the noise. Suddenly with an enormous bang the sphere vanished completely, and the room was plunged into darkness.

Slowly the espartano brothers stood up and peered around the side of the crate into the blackness, "squad firing positions!" the Majors voice echoed from across the room, shuffles could be heard as the platoon slowly got to their feet "who's out there?" Branigan called, "identify yourself or my men will open fire!", suddenly the rooms emergency lighting flicked on and in the center of the room two terrifying robotic figures could be seen stood side by side, in their arms they clutched identical gatling guns, the weapons lasers aimed directly at the officer's body, the whole platoon simultaneously gasped in shock as the two assault droids squeezed their triggers and unleashed a volley of bullets into the squad, Major Brannigan screamed as the depleted uranium bullets instantly thumped into his flesh, completely ripping his torso in two, Thaddeus and Ebenezer cheered from their cover and watched as the entire squad fell like dominoes, finally the shooting stopped, and smoke poured from the barrels of the gatling guns. Thaddeus and Ebenezer looked at each other "where the fuck did, they come from?" Thaddeus whispered. The assault droids turned to face them "get over here, hurry" the Blue camouflage droid droned to the brothers. Slowly the espartano brothers stood up and approached the assault droids, empty round casings rattled across the floor as they walked "who are you?" Thaddeus asked as they reached the droids "take a wild guess" the black camo robot answered, Thaddeus and Ebenezer looked at each other in confusion. "In a second Ebenezer, a voice is going to come through that headset" the blue droid announced, "when it does you must tell me and do exactly what I say", "alright" Ebenezer said with a confused tone "but how do you know that and who the fuck are you?", the black droid stepped forward and

124

put a mechanical hand on Ebenezer's shoulder "you tell me bro?" the droid asked, Thaddeus and Ebenezer looked at each other, "fuck me" they both said in unison.

The blast door slowly shut behind the brothers as they entered the room and Ebenezer could here the voice crackle into his ear once more, "Well, you wanted him, here he is, may I present to you...", "let me guess" Ebenezer interrupted "that's Klausner, has fucking dead and you (the dean of Oxford university) are about to blow this place to kingdom come, sounds about right doesn't it?", "yeah" Thaddeus replied standing to his feet "sounds about right", "what the!?" the dean bellowed through the rooms speakers, "what the fucks the meaning of this?, how did you survive the guards?", "well" Ebenezer said smugly as the shutter came up and the lights flickered on "we had some help". Suddenly the wall to the right of the dean exploded and the two mechanical espartano brothers charged in "arrghh, fucking unhand me!" the deans voice bellowed through the speakers as the mecha-brothers seized him. "tell us where the doctor is you piece of shit!" the robotic voice of Ebenezer bellowed as he slammed his cybernetic fist into the dean's ribcage, the dean screamed in pain as he chocked on blood "if I tell you, will you kill me quickly?" he spluttered. The two robots looked through the window at Thaddeus and Ebenezer who both grinned and shook their heads "no" Mecha- Thaddeus replied "but well make sure you go out with a bang" The robots grabbed an arm in each of there powerful robotic fists and as he screamed in agony the pair twisted his arms until they popped at the sockets "ok!!" he screamed "he's in a fucking ship, it's a fucking ship in the earths orbit", the brothers twisted his arms more until the flesh began to tear at the shoulders, the deans eyes were wide with panic as he bellowed in pain louder and louder, Thaddeus and Ebenezer stared in amusement through the glass as there cybernetic counterparts tortured the information out of the dean "man were badass in the future" Ebenezer said to Thaddeus through a beaming grin "what fucking ship!" Mecha-Thaddeus yelled into the dean's ear "its…it's the airship" the Dean whispered as he nearly fell unconscious through the pain "airship?" Mecha-Ebenezer quizzed "yes" he groaned "Jimmy Whizz sent the schematics through to the doctor before you could kill him, he's made one just like yours" "CORE MELTDOWN IN T-MINUS 3 MINUTES" a computerized warning suddenly bellowed from the rooms speakers "Thaddeus, Ebenezer" Mecha-Thaddeus

126

yelled through the rooms speakers "you need to get to the time portal, it will take you into the future, you must kill the doctor", "come with us!" Thaddeus yelled through the glass "negative, well stay here with pretty boy" Mecha-Ebenezer replied as he tore the Deans face off with his robotic hand, the Dean shrieked and writhed in agony, still in the grip of the robots "we can't survive together in the same timeline look!" he pointed at Thaddeus who looked down to see in horror that his body was starting to fade away beneath him "fuck!" he yelled, "get out of here now" Mecha-Thaddeus yelled through the speakers as he hit a button which opened the blast door "give our love to the crew". "CORE MELTDOWN IN T-MINUS 1 MINUTE" the computerized voice echoed through the room once more "we will, and thank you" Thaddeus said before the two brothers turned and sprinted out of the room and down the corridor. Mecha-Thaddeus and Ebenezer smiled to each other as they slowly ripped the dean completely in half, he screamed and begged even when the tearing reached his vocal cords the pitiful sobbing could still be heard.

"Goffbot!" Ebenezer yelled into his headset as the brothers scuttled their way back up the access corridor "Goffbot do you read me" "uhh loud and clear boss" the voice replied, "listen the crew need to get the airship space worthy, contact Mr. Red, hell get you what you need, do this one thing without fucking it up for once and your redeemed for every fuck up you ever made" "uhh yes boss" the voice replied, "CORE MELTDOWN IMMINENT" the voice announced through the speakers, the brothers emerged from the access hatch and ran as fast as they could at the slowly fading orb of electricity in the middle of the room "come on lets fucking move!" Thaddeus yelled, the room shook violently, and the two brothers jumped into the portal together.

CHAPTER 19: R.I.S.E.

Location: The "Hungry Bird" airship

Date: December 7th, 2043

Time: 22:30 hrs

"That was quicker than I expected" Core said as the two brothers crashed onto the deck of the Hungry Bird "glad your back to your old selves, those assault droids' feet left enormous dents in the airships floor" "did it work?" Ebenezer spluttered as he shakily stood to his feet "did you get my message?", "looks like the Goffbot came through for once" Core replied, "take a look out of the window "Thaddeus and Ebenezer gazed out of the window into space "fuck me" Thaddeus gasped "I take it the robot versions of us didn't survive the blast?" Ebenezer asked miserably "unfortunately not" Core replied, "but don't worry, I pulled there consciousness out and downloaded it somewhere "ahh not that fucking cabin!?" Thaddeus inquired "they'll never figure the door out" Core laughed "I put them in the same cabin as Fatty, I uploaded them as droids so they never hurt, they get to have a front row seat and watch him run around the room screaming all day as his flesh falls off, I'm in communication with them and when they finally get bored I'll put them somewhere else", "don't put me anywhere else" Thaddeus replied through a grin, "Id never get bored of that"

"TARGET AQUIRED, RED BARON AIRSHIP" a voice suddenly boomed through the airship's speakers, "fuckinghell what's that?" Ebenezer asked, "ah that's the Goffbot" Core replied, "he uploaded himself into the ships computer, hell of an upgrade if you ask me", "what the fucks the Red Baron?" Thaddeus asked "yeah" Core replied hesitantly "I believe the reason Jimmy whizz invaded the airship was to upload schematics to the doctor so he could make his own", "yeah I mentioned that to myself." Ebenezer muttered. "Tell me this thing has had a weapons upgrade?" Core smiled in response before directing his attention to a camera mounted in the upper right corner of the room.

"Computer, Ready the starboard cannons!" Core shouted, "oh and raise the shields it's a long way back down to earth, good shout Ebenezer replied nodding in agreement, SHIELDS AT 100%, LAZER CANNONS

LOADED AND READY AT YOUR COMMAND "roger!" Thaddeus yelled at the camera in response, as he rubbed his hands together "lets see just how hungry this fucking bird really is!" he said excitedly.

Thaddeus and Ebenezer watched in anticipation as the hellish red baron airship loomed into view "Goffbot!..err I mean computer" Thaddeus yelled "standby for my command!" "STANDING BY" the ships computer boomed in response.

Finally, the Hungry Bird crept alongside of the Red Baron and Thaddeus raised his hand high above his head. "Fire away!" Thaddeus commanded, a huge boom one after another rocked the airship side to side Ebenezer clapped and whooped as explosions scattered the hull of the Red Baron as the Hungry Birds cannon balls punched through its hull. Thaddeus joined in his brother's celebration, shoveling popcorn and whisky down his gullet, he grinned as they shared an appreciation of the destruction, "RED BARON SHIELDS CRITICAL" The ships computer informed them "fuck this is too easy" Thaddeus laughed.

Suddenly just as he finished his sentence there was an enormous bang that rocked the Hungry Bird so violently Ebenezer's popcorn went flying all over the place. "SHIELDS AT 50%", "what the fuck!" Thaddeus yelled "where the fuck did that come from?", another huge bang and the Hungry bird was nearly ripped in two by the Red Barons counterattack "SHIELDS AT 10%" the ships computer crackled. "Fuck! evasive maneuvers!" Ebenezer yelled "core!" Thaddeus called across the room "work on disabling the engines and find a way to take out there cannon, we can't take another hit!" "roger!" core replied, "Ebenezer get ready to board, we might not have much time!" Thaddeus yelled as the Hungry Bird dodged another devastating attack "Roger" Ebenezer replied as he scrambled on the floor trying to catch the rolling bottle of whiskey "there's spacesuits and jetpacks outside of the armory" Core informed Them as he jumped onto a nearby computer terminal. "There's an airlock in the cargo bay, I'll get the Barons engines offline, you get in there and do what you do best", "you got it!" Thaddeus replied as he caught the rolling bottle and threw it to Ebenezer, "lets fucking do this!" he roared.

The two brothers hurriedly threw on the spacesuits and jetpacks after which Ebenezer opened the armory doors "grab what you can bro!" he said as he

132

stuffed knuckle dusters and grenades into his cot vest. Thaddeus marched in and picked up a matching pair of silver Uzi's and slotted them into his hip holsters "alright let's go!" he said to Ebenezer. The two men left the room and headed down the corridor and into the elevator "computer, prepare to open the airlock" Thaddeus commanded as the elevator descended to the cargo bay. Ebenezer drew his machete and inspected the blade, "man I'm looking forward to cutting off this son of a bitches head" he grinned, "maybe we'll bring it back with us as a souvenir?" Thaddeus suggested, Ebenezer nodded gleefully as the elevator came to a stop on the cargo bay floor. The brothers made their way across the room to the large white airlock which had been installed next to the landing ramp "ok computer, open the airlock" Thaddeus instructed. Instantly the airlock opened with a hiss and the brothers stepped inside the door which closed behind them. "Ready?" Ebenezer asked as he drew his machete "ready!" Thaddeus replied.

"Computer, open the external airlock door." Ebenezer commanded, the external airlock door opened and the two brothers suddenly experienced zero gravity "whoa fuckinghell!" Thaddeus remarked as his feet left the floor. "Guys!" Core's voice crackled through the brother's headsets, "on your right arm there's thrust controls, use these to direct yourselves to the Red Baron", "roger" Thaddeus replied as he examined his glove, he pressed a green button and began to jet his way out of the airlock and into space "fuckinghell this thing's insane!" he called cheerfully, Ebenezer followed shortly after and the two men began the journey from the Hungry Bird toward the Red baron "look" Thaddeus's voice suddenly came through Ebenezer's helmet, Ebenezer looked at his brother and saw he was gesturing toward the moon, he looked and gasped as he saw what Thaddeus was pointing at. On the dark side of the moon stood an enormous structure which glowed a fantastic shade of blue "uhh Core, are you seeing this?" Ebenezer asked, "I see it" Core replied, "I'm scanning it now…fuck me, guys that's a fucking weapon, that's how the doctor is punching holes through the world without being detected, the attacks are coming from space!", "how do we destroy it?" Ebenezer called through the headset as the brothers approached the Red Barons airlock, "there must be a way of deactivating it inside the doctor's airship" Core replied "you've gotta get in there and take this son of a bitch out fast, that fucking thing looks like its charging up for another strike!", "fuck!"

Ebenezer yelled back as he attempted to engage the airlocks control panel. "Core can you get this door open the outside controls have been disabled", "give me a second" Core replied, "ah shit I've been locked out, this might take some time gents", Ebenezer looked down at his arm controls and noticed his suits oxygen level was at 20% "come on, get this fucking door open, our oxygen is getting low here", "Core!" Thaddeus said suddenly "is the Dr's ship an exact copy of the hungry bird?", "pretty much" Core replied "I mean he's got more advanced tech and weaponry, but the hull is a direct copy...why? Thaddeus looked at Ebenezer "the access panel!" he said hurriedly "fuck, good thinking bro, lets move" Ebenezer replied. The brothers made their way down to the belly of the Red Baron. "here" Thaddeus called as he located the airships access panel.

Ebenezer gripped the hatch's handle and pulled with all this strength but couldn't open it, Thaddeus got side by side with his brother "pull!" he shouted and they both pulled with all their strength, suddenly the access panel door flew open and the brothers were sucked into the airship. they fell to the ground as the hatch slammed shut beneath them. "Jesus!" Ebenezer said looking at his arm readout "I had 1% left!", "fuck me that was close!"

Thaddeus replied as he stood to his feet. "whoa!" he remarked as he surveyed the scene around him "what the fuck is this place?" Ebenezer stood up and looked around the room. Every wall was covered with wires and flesh which appeared to be alive, the stench was unbearable, there were large transparent cylindrical containers which covered areas of the cargo bay floor "what the fuck are these for?" Ebenezer asked as he approached the container nearest them. "Berserker" he read from a label on the tank, peering into the glass he noticed a large, disfigured humanoid, it was a mixture of twisted metal and burnt flesh which had been fused together. Its arms were nothing but huge shards of razor-sharp steel "bro look at this, the fucking lunatic is making killing machines in here" "Jesus" Thaddeus whispered as he joined Ebenezer in gazing into the glass "look at that" he exclaimed in horror as he pointed to the experiments face, it was nothing but a twisted mess of flesh and steel with two deep recess's for eye sockets and shards of metal for teeth "isn't that the prettiest thing you've ever seen?" Ebenezer asked, Thaddeus grinned in response "still prettier than your ex-wife bro" he replied, Ebenezer laughed loudly and slapped his thigh, suddenly from inside the container two large bubbles rose from the floor of the chamber "whoa" Ebenezer said quietly "what was that?" he peered once more into the container and squinted at the creature's face. Suddenly the two eye sockets glowed a violent shade of red and electrical currents shot through the tank "fuck!" Ebenezer yelled as he jumped backwards "that can't be good!" Thaddeus replied as the creature began thrashing wildly inside of the tank, "get ready!" Ebenezer yelled as he drew his machete, Thaddeus pulled out one of his Uzis from its holsters and drew his own machete, the brothers waited anxiously to engage the creature but finally after a couple of minutes the movement stopped and the brothers cautiously stepped forward to investigate, Ebenezer peered once more inside the tank which was now thick with a mixture of blood and oil "huh" he exclaimed as he looked at Thaddeus "maybe this Doctor asswipe isn't as smart as he thinks he is". Suddenly with a loud crash a spiked arm smashed through the tank just inches from Ebenezer's head "fuck!" he yelled as the Berserker ripped its way through the glass and stomped out onto the garage floor towering above them. It raised its spiked arms high above its head and let out a malevolent whirr as it slowly approached them "fuck me!" Thaddeus yelled as he aimed his Uzi at its head.

137

CHAPTER 20: BY APPOINTMENT ONLY

Location: The "Red Baron" airship

Date: December 7th, 2043

Time: 23:00 hrs

Thaddeus unloaded the entire magazine from his Uzi into the Berserkers face, bullets ripped into its flesh and sparks flew everywhere but it was no use, the Berserker continued its approach toward the brothers and began swinging its spiked limbs violently, from around the room Thaddeus noticed that other nightmarish experiments began tearing their way out of their tanks "shit bro we gotta do something, bullets don't do shit against these things!" he pulled the other Uzi from his holster and unleashed another full magazine into the creatures torso, dead blood and oil spurted from the Berserkers body but again made no impact in slowing its approach. Slowly the brothers were being pushed into a corner as the other creatures began advancing on them too.

"fuck fuck!" Ebenezer yelled as he looked desperately around the room. "There!" Thaddeus yelled as he pointed in the direction of a control panel in the corner of the cargo bay. Ebenezer pulled a grenade from his chest rig, pulling the pin he threw the grenade across the room just as the creatures closed in on the brothers.

With a loud bang the control panel exploded, and sparks flew across the garage, The Berserker drew back its spiked arms ready to thrust them directly into Thaddeus when suddenly the redness faded from its eye sockets and it slumped to the floor with a crash just inches from where the brothers were standing, one by one the other experiments did the same. Ebenezer took a deep breath and looked at Thaddeus who had a metal spike just millimeters from his face. "let's find this mother fucker" Thaddeus said slowly. Ebenezer helped him to his feet and the two brothers made there way across the room and into the elevator. "what are these things?" Thaddeus asked as the elevator began its ascent "I don't know" Ebenezer replied as he removed his helmet "but this Doctor must be a fucking psychopath, we have to stop him bro", Thaddeus nodded in agreement as he removed his own helmet.

The elevator stopped and before the doors could open, they were ripped from their hinges from the outside "fuck!" yelled Thaddeus, in the doorway stood a huge 7ft cyborg, for a split second the brothers stood in awe of the terrifying machine before them, suddenly the cyborg charged into the elevator smashing directly into Thaddeus and pinning him against the elevator wall "arrghhh!" he yelled as the cyborg grasped Thaddeus's throat with a steel claw and began to squeeze "fuck you, you stainless steel son of a bitch!" Ebenezer yelled as he started smashing it in the back of the head with Reggie Krays knuckle duster "fucking let go!" Ebenezer unsheathed his machete and thrusted it with all of his might into the base of the cyborg's skull, Ebenezer twisted his machete as hard as he could when suddenly a loud bang filled the elevator as he wrenched its skull completely off its body, "get this fucker off me!" Thaddeus gasped as Ebenezer removed the claw from his brother's throat. "You ok?" Ebenezer asked "fine" Thaddeus replied through a cough "thanks", "no problem" Ebenezer replied "come on, get your shit together, lets end this". Thaddeus stood up and let out a terrifying war cry before marching out of the elevator and into the Red Baron's corridor.

Another two grotesque cyborgs stood between the brothers and the door to the doctor's office at the end of the corridor. "Fuck we've got no choice" Thaddeus mumbled still trying to find his voice "we have to fight through", "we can do this bro" Ebenezer replied licking blood from his machetes blade "lets fucking kill these assholes." The two brothers ran down the corridor bellowing at the top of there lungs as they collided with the two enormous creatures.

The brothers let loose with all they had, violently attacking the cyborgs with immense force, their machetes swooshed and sliced through the air, cutting chunks of flesh and metal off as they engaged the enemies. Finally, all that remained of the creatures was a huge pile of flesh and metal, Thaddeus wiped blood and oil from his face "let's get this son of a bitch" he gasped as he cleaned his machete's blade on his trouser leg.

The brothers had reached the door at the end of the corridor, Thaddeus noticed a brass plaque on the wall: "DR G Webster MD" he read out loud "this is it bro, get ready" Suddenly a robot voice came over a speaker system.

"THE DOCTOR WILL SEE YOU NOW"

CHAPTER 21: RAGE AGAINST THE MACHINE.

Location: The "Red Baron" airship

Date: December 7th, 2043

Time: 00:00 hrs

The steel doors slid open to reveal a dimly lit office, the two brothers stepped inside, their machetes drawn and dripping with flesh and oil. The room was filled from floor to ceiling with what appeared to be failed lab experiments. Thaddeus put his hand to his mouth to mask the stench of rotting flesh fused with metal. In the centre of the room was a gorgeous leather topped mahogany writing desk, the desktop itself was covered with crystal ashtrays and dot-matrix printers that whirred away annoyingly as they churned out sheets of paper. Behind the desk stood a large red velvet armchair, its back toward the brothers. "Bro look!" Thaddeus said suddenly pointing to a curl topped coat stand in a corner of the room "fuckinghell!" Ebenezer loudly replied his jaw almost hitting the floor. A luxury red dinner jacket swung from one of the clothes hooks and Thaddeus and Ebenezer looked at each other in shock, suddenly a slow clap could be heard from behind the armchair followed by a familiar voice: "gentlemen" Mr. Red cooed smoothly as he stood up from the armchair and faced the brothers "may I offer you a victorious glass of scotch?", "what…what are you doing here?" Ebenezer gasped as Mr. Red opened a draw in the desk and produced a bottle of fine liquor and three crystal glasses, "take a seat" he said calmly gesturing to the two armchairs on the opposite side of the desk. Cautiously Thaddeus and Ebenezer crossed the room and slumped simultaneously into the chairs their machetes still clutched in their hands "here" he said handing the brothers a glass each, "may I propose a toast to your victory", "what victory?!" Ebenezer replied angrily suddenly jumping to his feet. "ah that's better" Mr. Red replied to the action "never toast sitting down" he clinked his glass to Ebenezer's and took a generous gulp of the delicious beverage. Ebenezer did not return the compliment "Answer my fucking question!" he demanded "what the fuck are you doing here? And do you have control over that monstrosity on the moon?" Thaddeus stood up and chucked the whiskey down his gullet before throwing his glass against the office wall

143

"start talking!" he said as he raised his machete. "Gentlemen relax" Mr. Red replied calmly as he placed the empty glass on the table "please sit back down and allow me to explain". Begrudgingly the brothers returned to the seated position. "Oh, how rude of me, I almost forgot to offer you a cigar" Mr. Red pulled a leather cigar wallet from his jacket and withdrew two Lord Winterbells. "here" he said as he passed one each to the brothers "Thanks" Ebenezer replied coldly "now start fucking talking" Mr. Red smiled to himself and took a seat in his armchair, crossing his legs and lighting his cigar he began to talk. "What do you both know about the organisation known as R.I.S.E?" Thaddeus shrugged his shoulders "not a lot, all we know is that in the late 20th century the organisation was classed as having a terroristic agenda and was subsequently shut down by the government" Mr. Red let out a small chuckle and proceeded to pour himself another whiskey "care for a refill gentleman?" he offered the brothers. Ebenezer necked the contents of his glass and smashed the empty vessel into his cranium "no, you crack on" he said firmly, "fair enough" Mr. Red replied stuffing the cork back into the bottle. "sorry as you were saying Thaddeus", "That's all we know" Thaddeus replied folding his arms "well"

Mr. Red continued what if I told you that the reason R.I.S.E was shut down was because the organisation had developed time travel technology, and all those greedy pen pushers in the government couldn't wait to get their hands on it" Thaddeus and Ebenezer gazed back at Mr. Red clearly unimpressed, "so?" Ebenezer muttered "what's that got to do with you?", "I'll tell you" Mr. Red replied a tone of anger in his voice, "my father was the head of R.I.S.E and a genius if you will, it was him alone who developed time travel capability and those barbaric T.R.E.K.K operatives broke down the doors and slaughtered him and every one of his staff members in cold blood, just so they could steal his technology" Mr. Red slumped back into his armchair and took a long draw from his cigar "I was just a boy hiding under a desk when a T.R.E.K.K operative broke down the doors, I watched as my father begged for his life before being shot in front of me" Ebenezer yawned loudly and let out a burp at the apex, Mr. Red gave him a disgusted look and cleared his throat "for hours I hid amongst the ruins of my father's workshops surrounded by dead bodies and hearing only the screams of the wounded. Finally, T.R.E.K.K sent in their combat medics and one of them found and took pity on me, her name was Mya, you might already know her?" Mr. Red grinned as he sipped his glass. Thaddeus and Ebenezer looked at each other in bewilderment. "Ah, now I believe I have your attention Ebenezer?" Mr. Red continued, "Mya raised me to become an operative within T.R.E.K.K and when I was ready, they used the captured time travel technology to send me back to assassinate high profile targets, every week a new name would appear on the list, Id jump through the portal and find myself standing in an opera house with a derringer, or outside of a book depository with a sniper rifle" suddenly Mr. Red stood to his feet and leant across the table "or I could even find myself outside the doors to R.I.S.E HQ with a mission to kill the leader, that's right they sent me on a mission to kill my own father, and the worst part was that I didn't even remember who he was. As the years went by, I rose to become the head of T.R.E.K.K and finally discovered the horrific truth. I vowed from that moment forward I would continue my father's work and destroy anyone who got it my way, for example one e-mail from the united states department of energy was enough for me to consider them a threat, a threat which had to be neutralised" Ebenezer leapt to his feet once more shaking in anger "so it was you? It was you who wiped out an entire country? you killed half a million people!" Mr. Red chuckled to himself once more "I believe it's called collateral damage?" he said smugly. "Ill show you fucking collateral damage!" Ebenezer roared as he smashed his fist into the nearest dot matrix printer sending it whirring across the desk to its imminent death. Thaddeus stood up and drew his machete once more "I don't give a fuck about your sob story you piece of shit; you're fucking dead", "gentleman!" Mr. Red reasoned "you must understand what we can accomplish together, all of the people who stood in your way, the Dean, Langley, all of them were just a test, a list I made of the most challenging of adversaries just to prove that the only ones worthy to stand beside me were you two, together we will be unstoppable, I sent Core who by the way was my masterpiece, the components to build the time machine but I only sent him what was required for one trip, with the technology I possess we can use it indefinitely, we can travel wherever and whenever we want, think about it gentleman, the world will be at your mercy" Thaddeus and Ebenezer looked at each other and grinned broadly "well?" Mr. Red said excitedly as he looked anxiously at two brothers "what do you say?", Ebenezer looked at Thaddeus and leaned over the desk toward Mr. Red "I say fuck you" he replied through a grin. "you can take your plans for world domination and shove them up your ass" Mr. Red slumped back down into his armchair and took another gulp of whiskey "how disappointing" he said flatly as he pulled a silver detonator from his waistcoat pocket "what are you going to do with that?" Thaddeus laughed "blow us up? been there done that". Mr. Red let out a sinister chuckle, "gentlemen would you be so kind as to direct your attention to the window and more notably your precious airship", Ebenezer leapt up and hurried to the office window, Thaddeus followed. "last chance" Mr. Red spoke again "your either with me or against me", "go fuck yourself!" Thaddeus yelled, Mr. Red smiled smugly and hit the switch. The brothers watched in horror as the moon weapon slowly lined its enormous barrel up with the Hungry Bird "Core!" Ebenezer yelled into his headset "you need to get the fuck out of here hes going to…" suddenly Ebenezer stopped short and watched as an enormous beam of blue laser smashed into the side of the Hungry Bird and obliterated it into a billion pieces.

"NOOOOOOOO!!!" the brothers yelled at the top of there lungs, "you son of a bitch, your fucking dead!" Ebenezer roared as he strode across the room

148

towards Mr. Red. "save some for me!" Thaddeus barked as he headed toward the other side of Mr. Reds desk. Ebenezer slammed his enormous fist into Mr. Reds torso so hard he ripped clean through the skin and his knuckles felt the slimy texture of Mr. Reds intestines, he grabbed hold of them and ripped them out with all his might. Mr. Red screamed at the top of his lungs and fell to the floor "you fools" he gasped as he choked on his own blood "now we will all die together". Still clutching the silver detonator, he hit the switch once more "SELF DESTRUCT SEQUENCE INITIATED" a voice boomed from the ship's computers. Mr. Red let out a sickening laugh "gentlemen it's been a pleasure as always" he spat.

"Really, the pleasure was all ours" Ebenezer replied through pure anger as he picked up a dot matrix printer and smashed it into Mr. Reds skull.

CHAPTER 22: RED MIST.

Location: The "Red Baron" airship

Date: December 8th, 2043

Time: 00:30 hrs

"SHIP WILL SELF DESTRUCT IN T-MINUS 3 MINUTES" Ebenezer and Thaddeus looked at each other "well, there goes our ride home" Thaddeus said miserably as he observed from the window the Hungry Birds wreckage suspended in space. "Yup" Ebenezer replied, "might as well make the most of it".

Ebenezer yanked open Mr. Reds desk draw and uncorked the bottle of whiskey, the walls began to shake around him as he took a huge gulp "well" he said cheerfully as he offered the bottle to his brother, "it's not like this hasn't happened before".

Thaddeus nodded as he took the bottle and together, they looked out of the window "to the crew" Thaddeus said "to the crew" Ebenezer replied joining him in the toast. "Wait!" Ebenezer said suddenly "what did you just say?", "what?" Thaddeus replied, "to the crew?", "no not that, what did you say before?", Thaddeus looked confused "it's not like this hasn't happened before?", he replied, "yes!" Ebenezer shouted excitedly "this did happen before, the nuclear power plant remember? how did we change things then?", "uhh time travel?" Ebenezer nodded and headed toward the door "what's the plan?" Thaddeus asked as he followed Ebenezer "Mr. Red must have a time machine of his own and it must be on this ship, come on we've got to find it!"

"SHIP WILL SELF DESTRUCT IN T-MINUS 1 MINUTE" the ships computer boomed again.

Thaddeus and Ebenezer ran down the ship's corridor kicking in the doors of every room as they went, around them the ships hull began to break apart "here!" Ebenezer yelled at a door marked Time travel room "this is it!", "you think?" Thaddeus replied sarcastically, Ebenezer booted the door down and the brothers ran inside the room "fuck what do we do?" Ebenezer yelled as he studied the time displacement chamber and control unit that stood next to it "fuck I don't know!" Thaddeus yelled over the explosions coming from within the ship.

"SHIP WILL SELF DESTRUCT IN T-MINUS 10 SECONDS"

"Fuck" Thaddeus yelled "just fucking press everything!", Ebenezer ran up to the control panel and started jabbingbuttons wildly.

"TIME SEQUENCE INITIATED" a computerised voice spoke "PLEASE ENTER DESTINATION" Ebenezer frantically began smashing the living daylights out of the control panel. "bro we don't have any time, this place is about to blow!" Thaddeus yelled as he grabbed Ebenezer and pulled him into the displacement chamber with him.

"SHIP WILL NOW SELF DESTRUCT"

There was an enormous bang and then darkness.

CHAPTER 23: THE EAGLE HAS FALLEN.

Location: Berlin

Date: August 1st, 1936

Time: 0900 hrs

Thaddeus opened his eyes and felt dirt beneath him "bro" he asked weakly, "are we fucking dead again?", "god I hope not" Ebenezer coughed as he replied, "I can't bear to go back to that fucking cabin" The two brothers stood to their feet and looked around them in amazement "where the fuck are we?" Thaddeus gasped.

Rows of seats completely filled the stadium and the thousands of people who sat on them them had gone completely silent as they witnessed the brother's arrival "fuckinghell" Ebenezer remarked, "look!" he pointed towards the entrance of the stadium at the huge Olympic rings that surrounded it "holy shit!" Thaddeus replied gleefully "were at the fucking Olympic games!" The brothers looked around the stadium and bowed to the crowds who responded with a large round of applause at their grand entrance. "bro look!" Thaddeus pointed "everyone's here! look at all the flags, theres Britain and America and... hang on, is that a fucking swastika?" Ebenezer looked at the huge Nazi flag which hung in the centre of the stadium "uhh, bro I think I know where we are" Ebenezer said quietly "this is the fucking Berlin Olympics".

From overhead a loud buzzing could be heard. The two brothers looked up just in time to see an enormous airship looming into view above the stadium "what the fuck is that?" Thaddeus asked. "das ist die Hindenburg" a voice suddenly called from behind them, the brothers span around and came face to face with a tall blonde Aryan featured man dressed from head to toe in green lycra with a swastika on his chest. "ya, ya est ist wunderbar ya?", Thaddeus rubbed his hands together "mmm very wunderbar indean!" he replied as he watched the glorious airship float past. "Heil Hitler!" The man suddenly shouted and performed a perfect bellamy salute. "uhh yeah whatever" Ebenezer grunted. The man gave the brothers a strange look and continued his running down the track. "did he say...?" Thaddeus began "heil fucking Hitler" Ebenezer replied with a shocked look on his face "bro look!" he pointed toward the stadiums entrance and the two brothers watched with open mouths as Adolf Hitlers Mercedes Benz entered the stadium followed by an entourage of black Volkswagen beetles "Fuck me!" Thaddeus yelled "its fucking Hitler!", the two brothers unsheathed their machetes and began striding across the turf as the king of assholes himself began walking up to a podium draped in Nazi flags "dibs on that bonnet" Ebenezer exclaimed. The crowd stood to their feet and clapped as the brothers began to run.

The end.

Written by

Lord Thaddeus & Lord Ebenezer

22/02/2021

Printed in Great Britain
by Amazon